Fearless

a novel

Benjamin Warner

ISBN: 9781087896397

Published September 2022 by Malarkey Books
malarkeybooks.com

Cover design by Matt Muirhead
Typesetting by Alan Good

"To provoke fear, we exposed her to live snakes and spiders, took her on a tour of a haunted house, and showed her emotionally evocative films."

—"The Human Amygdala and the Induction and Experience of Fear," *Current Biology,* December 2010

There were always stories about the fires. In the papers, on the news desks—discussed in the hands-on-hips style endemic to our small city-lawns. At first, the police were baffled. But theories emerged: faulty wiring, pyromania, even bombings. There were whispers of self-infliction, too—insurance payouts that business owners collected as the migration to the suburbs came to bear. Others said it was only in a place like our city that spontaneous combustion could still be possible—that our particular variety of wan sunlight might be trapped inside those brick rowhouses for such long periods of disuse that it would burst through the windows in flame.

But the discrepancies in the stories were so wide as to make them seem hollow, and the good people of our city didn't pay them any serious mind. It was, they eventually concluded, simply a phenomenon.

I was just a little girl.

I remember during those first fires—the Channel 4 news breaking in through evening game shows—my mother saying to me, "You see, Christine? You see why we don't have that stove anymore? Your father wasn't so horrible to get rid of it." She hadn't liked the wounded tone with which I'd been pestering my father about removing the wood-burning stove from our living room. "I don't like the wounded tone you've been pestering your father with," she told me. "People's houses are burning down from a lot less. And look what it did to you. Hold still, Christine. Hold still." She'd been struggling to unwrap the bandages from my hand, to put on a fresh coat of antiseptic cream. Our stove had been in the corner of the living room, and it was just a week before that I'd been captivated by its heat. What I remember is that it felt like gravity, a force that pulled down on the tangle of my brain in an attempt to untie all its complicated knots. What was a net of gray matter wanted only to become a limp noodle pointing in a single direction. I was not an infant. I knew that my hand, reaching to touch that stove, would be burned, and that in the course of that burn I would experience pain. But when I touched it, the pain came back as something else. Dr. Blau says I replace those sensations with "precursory experiences," so that all I feel is heat. It's true that I didn't feel the terrible searing of my flesh, but instead a spreading and delicious warmth inside me.

When the fires started up again, years later, no one tried to explain them. Maybe people had never stopped living in the memory—when smoke was always on the horizon—and so were inured to their return. It was interesting. Carl said to me, "You were at the site where it started, right? You and this doctor guy? It's not *you* starting the fires. Do the math, Christine."

But it can't be Dr. Blau. His budget is on a shoestring this year, and our methods must be cheap: these free association memory journals, the self-affect log book. How many of *those* have I gone through? When I ask Dr. Blau if he's ready to analyze the data, he tells me we need to continue building the sample. "Even a sample size of *one*," he tells me, "is infinitely more instructive than a sample size of zero."

Just once, he means, I have to be afraid. Just once, I have to record a legitimate fear response in the log book.

One simple, terrifying memory in my free association entries. I suppose that I could lie. Save us all the trouble. But wouldn't that tarnish all the work we've done?

There's the list of phobias we've checked off, for instance—each potential terror with its varieties, its gradients, degrees. It's never as simple as just "Spiders." I've tried orb-weavers and wolfs and hobos and those Brazilian ones that jump. We have 33,996 species to go, but we've crossed <u>Item 3</u>, *Arachnophobia* off our list. "For now," says Dr. Blau, "the tests we *have* will have to do."

When the fires came back this second time, Dr. Blau got as hopeful as a kid. We were in the lab, watching it on the news, flames poking out a third-story window. *The cause of the blaze,* the reporter said, *is still unknown.*

Dr. Blau had rubbed his hands together. He'd whooped, which he hardly ever does.

"The cause?" he'd whooped. "Who cares about the cause? What we've got is a perfect experiment."

"I don't know," I said.

"You don't know? You don't know, Jenny?"

"Christine," I corrected him. Sometimes, when Dr. Blau gets excited, his passions mix him up.

But it usually clears up quickly.

"We'll take you to the fires, Christine! Imagine. Inside each fire, there are people who need to be saved. And people don't live in the same place very long without gathering precious things. There will be precious things to save, too, Christine! And all the while you'll be self-affect rating in your log."

"You want me to go inside the burning buildings," I said, just to get it straight.

"And how does that make you feel?" he said. "Tut-tut. Get it out."

I did. I rated all my affects in the log book. My alertness was a 7. My angst was at a 3. But my fear was still a Ø.

Dr. Blau put the stethoscope to my chest to listen for heart palpitations. He held open my eye with his thumb and forefinger to see if my pupils had dilated. "How about your arms?" he said. "Raise them up. Do they feel like ineffectual tubes of air?"

I raised up my arms. They felt made of muscle and bone, not at all like tubes of air.

Dr. Blau made a note. "Okay," he said. "A negative result at the mere suggestion of a fire. That's a baseline we can work with. Now let's get you to the real thing."

As we turn onto the block, I can see the fire vibrating up ahead. It's a beacon, lighting our way through the darkness of the night.

"Okay," says Dr. Blau, looking at me from the driver's seat. "Officer P.J. Young says it's an eighty-three-year-old man and his live-in nurse."

A second-story rowhouse, connected at the shoulders to a whole silent block. One vigilant window, lifted up in flame. We get out and stand on the broken sidewalk. Flames against the winter sky, yet the winter sky is black. The fire casts no light above. It's only in his hand that Dr. Blau's notepad flickers.

"How do you feel?" he says.

I nod my head and pucker my lips to show him that I'm ready.

"This looks like a hot one. You may be horribly burned. I may not be able to save you."

"Okay," I say, knowing that if what he says is true, I will not be okay.

He hands me the lump hammer and folds the report back into his pocket. "Remember, you're looking for an eighty-three-year-old. *And* a live-in nurse. Though I get the feeling it might be a life partner. P.J. Young can be squeamish about these things."

"Squeamish?" I say.

"I want you to try for both, Christine. Don't make any hard choices between the two. Dally if you have to. Take your time and really search. It will be hard to see with all the smoke. It will be hard to breathe."

"And what if the fire's already got them?"

"Then you're only rescuing corpses." He pats me on the shoulder and gives me a weighty look. "Makes for a more meaningful funeral, having the bodies there. Just keep telling yourself that, Christine."

I get up to the first floor door and knock. It's 3 a.m., and I get no answer. I knock again, and this time I keep it up. A man wearing silk pajamas opens. He looks at the lump hammer in my hand.

"It's 3 a.m.," he says.

"I know," I say. "I'm sorry. But your top apartment is on fire."

He comes out on the stoop with me and cranes his neck.

"Sweet Jesus," he says. "There's an eighty-three-year-old man and his life partner who live up there. Call the fire department!"

"Everything's cool," says Dr. Blau, holding up his hand. "The authorities have been made aware."

I walk up the steps to the second-floor apartment. Smoke is coming from the crack beneath the door.

I knock.

"Anybody home?" I say. "You've got a bad situation in there."

I listen for the sound of eighty-three-year-old feet shuffling, for the sound of life-partner-feet shuffling, but all I hear is glass exploding. I take the lump hammer and bang around the knob until the wood splinters and the door swings open wide.

The smoke comes at me like the ghost of a person I've wronged. I'm enveloped and coughing, and hit the deck.

The smoke is weaker on the floor and I do a military crawl past the kitchen. Flames twist like copulating snakes up the casing of the doors. I feel the heat enter my skin, twisting around my arms and chest, and then inside, surrounding my heart and lungs. It is a mesmerizing heat. Like when I was a girl, swaddled in towels, bathed and clean, my father plunking me down in a little rocker in front of that wood-burning stove, saying, "You stay put, now. You just sit there and bake, Miss Potato." Just like before I went and ruined everything.

Even now I have to force myself to stop, to keep myself from moving closer and closer to the flames, from feeling this numbing pleasure before it turns to pain. My brain must be warped in more ways than we know.

I remember when we started these experiments, Dr. Blau took me to his lab and gave me ice cream. "Strawberry," he said, "right? I had a hunch. My daughter's a strawberry fanatic." He'd been so sweet. "We need," he'd said, "a place to start. Close your eyes. Imagine you're afraid. Imagine that you *could* be. Really try, Christine. What are you thinking of?"

"Fire," I'd said, but only because I'd been thinking of fire before he'd asked the question.

"Fire," he said. "Hmm. Haven't had one of those in a while."

That was after the early burnings, when everything went cool for a while.

From down on my belly, I reach to touch the flames around the door, my fingers almost glowing. I could radiate here forever, dissolve into an ember and forget all this ever happened.

But Dr. Blau disturbs me. "Rate!" I hear him shouting from below. "Make sure you remember to rate!"

I take the log book from out of my pocket and wrap my fingers around a pen.

Self-Rated Affect Log, 3:03 AM
Tranquility: 5
Exhilaration due to Rescue: 3
Pride: 1
Fear: ∅

I crawl into the bedroom. The old man's up on the bed, snoring. That means he's not unconscious yet.

"Hey," I say. "Hey!" and reach up to rattle his foot.

"Wha? What the heck?"

"Sir!" I say, "Sir, there's been a fire. I'm here to get you out."

He coughs like he's polishing rocks inside his chest.

"Where's your life partner?" I ask.

"My wha?"

"Life partner."

"Bill? Try the bathtub."

"Okay," I say, getting to my knees and pulling him by his ankles. I use his legs as a lever to get him sitting up straight on the bed.

"Hey," he says. "What is this? You're a lady."

"I'm stronger than I look," I say. "Come on now. Climb aboard."

"What are you," he says, "Good Samaritan or something? You ain't no FD."

"I'm running a series of tests to see whether or not I'm capable of experiencing fear," I say. "There's a scientist downstairs taking notes."

"Yeah," he says. "I think I heard a that."

"Just for the sake of the study," I say. "Let me ask you a question: How are you feeling right now?" Overhead, the fire laps the ceiling like a tide coming in.

"At my age, I was kinda hoping it would get me. It's no fun getting old."

I turn around and hold his wrists around my neck, take a deep breath and stand up wobbling. I've been practicing my lifts at the lab, holding my breath and hoisting the water jugs that Dr. Blau fills with coins.

"Yee-haw," he says. "What a night this turned out to be."

Outside, I try to be careful, but I drop him in a pile. Lucky for him, there's snow.

"Sorry," I say.

Dr. Blau takes me by the arm.

"There's another one up there," I say. "The life partner."

"Old Bill'll sleep through anything," says the geezer from his seat. "Ain't no rush on him."

Dr. Blau doesn't seem to hear. He has his checklist out.

"Weakness in the knees?" he says.

I shake my head.

"Shallowness of breath?"

"No."

"Heart palpitations? Pupil dilations?"

I go back up and crawl to the bathtub. I don't have much time before the sirens come.

"Bill?" I say. "Bill?"

"Yoo-hoo, Sweetheart," comes a voice.

I pull myself to the edge of the tub and see a man in there no more than thirty-five. He has wavy hair and an unbuttoned Hawaiian shirt.

His eyes are closed, but he pops them open like a Halloween trick, as if to make me flinch. The smoke overhead has the flat base of a placid summer cloud. "Don't I know you from my dreams?" he says. "Am I dreaming now?"

"Rise and shine if you are," I say. "House is on fire."

"Lord, lord. You *are* hot stuff. You must be the prettiest thing on this whole block, I swear. And I'd know. I seen 'em all."

I say, "Bill? How you feeling? You ready to crawl out of here with me?"

"Oh, I *could*. I certainly *could* . . . but come on, Sweetheart. I saw how you let Walter ride your back."

I pull on his arms and his body comes up squid-limp. Once he's aboard, he breathes into my ear.

"Aren't you just the bravest," he says. "Aren't you my little hero."

"I'm not brave," I say. "I'm not a hero."

"Oh no? Could've fooled me."

"You have to be afraid first. I'm not capable of that. At least that's what we think. Being afraid makes a difference. What are you afraid of now?"

"Right now?"

"Yeah."

"Being burnt up like a sausage link unless you get a move on."

"See," I say, "that doesn't bother me at all."

"Well, I'm happy for you. Honest, I am. Hee-yah!" he yells, digging his heels into my flanks. "Hee-yah!"

Just then, the ceiling collapses. A beam on fire lands at my feet.

"Isn't this my luck," Bill says. "Just when everything was going so well."

I arch backward and slough him back into the tub. I rip the curtain off the rod and soak it beneath the faucet.

"Come off it already," says Bill. "Let's just die."

He curls into a ball beneath a bottle of dandruff shampoo. I see the side of his chest rising harshly up and down.

"Don't worry," I say. "I've seen this happen before. I know what to do."

I take the wet curtain and throw it over the pile of flaming debris.

"C'mon," I say. "Let's try it one more time."

He climbs back on, and I get him down the stairs, into the snow next to Walter.

As Dr. Blau takes my readings, the two of them look up at me like puppies from a box.

"Rate," says Dr. Blau to me as he connects The Portable to my skull. "Rate!"

I rate.

Self-Rated Affect Log, 3:23 AM
Satisfaction: 2
Anger: 2
Elation: ∅
Fear: ∅

Walter cocks his head and scrunches up his nose. "I think it got you a little," he says, waggling a finger at my face. "I think you got a little cooked."

I touch the scar that runs as smooth as marble at my hairline.

"No," I say. "That's from before."

"Damn shame," he says. "Good looking gal like you."

I hold up my palm to show him what's left of my earliest burn, the one from touching the stove.

I say, "My mother could smell me burning all the way down the block."

Dr. Blau steps in between us. "He doesn't need to know all that. You saved his life," he says. "Isn't that enough?"

The downstairs neighbor in silk pajamas has stepped into galoshes. He blows into his hands.

"What the hell happened up there?" he asks them.

"Don't wet yourself with pity, Terrence," says Bill. "*You'll* get yours someday."

It's then we hear the sirens. Up the block the rowhouses flash red and blue before we see them come, their horrible horns set to break up all the traffic even though there's no traffic this time of night.

The FD hauls us back and gives us blankets. They stretch their yellow tape across the sidewalk. By the time the cops arrive, the place is doused, and in a couple of hours, the whole thing will be a cube of ice.

"Nothing," Dr. Blau is saying, observing the printout from The Portable. "No fear response at all. Did you really get into it up there? Did you allow yourself to get close to the flames?"

Officer P.J. Young has responded to the call, though I know it's not his shift. He's curious about our results.

"Anything?" he says, whispering, coming up close behind Dr. Blau.

"A negative event," says Dr. Blau.

"You're just too brave, Christine," Officer P.J. Young says to me.

I bite my tongue. Beneath the lights of all the emergency vehicles, the ground looks like a snow cone. Officer P.J. Young regards his shoes.

When the mess is cleaned up and the cops and FD have all gone home, and Walter and Bill are tucked away in some emergency shelter on the other side of town, Dr. Blau says, "Don't worry. We have other things to try. You'll see. There's a whole world out there of potentially frightening things."

"What about your 'viable experiment?'" I ask.

"You think that's the last of our burning buildings? Besides, maybe we're wrong about the fires. Maybe it's roller coasters you're afraid of. Stranger things, believe me. Speaking of which, it's late. You should be hitting the hay. We've got an important day tomorrow. You up for it? The Big Devil. I hear it has a nasty drop."

The Big Devil is the crown jewel of *Bang For Your Buck*, the new amusement park outside the Beltway . . . but how much more can we try? Each time we cross an item off the list, it's like pulling out a gray hair. They only seem to multiply, and it shows the sloppiness of our method. Tomorrow, we might eliminate "Roller Coasters," but really, it will only be the Big Devil that we know for sure. It could be that I'm afraid of the Demon, the Ghost, or the Freak.

I glance at Dr. Blau and try to look hopeful.

"A sampling will have to do," he says, when really, what we want is it all.

Then there was the time my father ended up with only four fingers on his right hand. Four and a half, really, and we probably could have saved the part above the knuckle if we weren't so deep into the woods. That was when my parents began to notice something strange. Most likely, it was *why* they noticed it. We were camping, of all things. We never camped. We weren't that kind of family. But something got into my father's head. He'd watched a special on the Smoky Mountains, and off we went—all that gear, "a real adventure," he called it. The seams on our packs were straining, and we hiked five miles on the trail to make our camp. It was that five-mile hike that did the finger in.

My father was all of a sudden a wildlife fanatic.

"Stop," he'd say. "Freeze," and my mother and I would stand where we were on the trail. "Do you hear that?" We'd listened to hours of bird calls on cassette tapes driving down. "A warbler . . . no . . . a chickadee." We'd walk some more, and he'd say, "Freeze!" again, and we'd wait while he inspected a pattern in the sticks. "Snake tracks," he'd say, bending so that his pack almost tipped him over. "No . . . deer more likely, white-tailed deer."

At the site, my mother and I unfolded the tent poles, while my father cooked on a white-gas stove. He'd wrapped a roast in cellophane. Eventually, my mother and I came to watch it hiss. "Eat, eat," my father urged when it was ready. We sat on rocks and held plastic plates on our laps. We ate, but we couldn't eat it all. "Stuff it in," my father said, seeing that we weren't going to finish. "Christine, try burping. Your problem is that you're full of air." Half the roast was left. That was our mistake. But what did we know about camping? We were city people.

By 8 o'clock, we'd gone into the tent, though the sun was up past 9. The five-mile hike had wiped us out. A little while later, we heard the baby shrieking. My mother and father were playing cards, sitting cross-legged in front of the mosquito-netting door. I was in my sleeping bag, staring at the fabric of our ceiling, watching it go from blue to gray, and then start to fade to black. "You hear that baby shrieking?" my father said. He was always afraid of noises. Tree limbs on the side of our house would send him prowling around with a baseball bat. The shrieks were getting louder.

"Oh dear lord," said my mother. I'd never seen her face like that. "They're killing it."

"Killing what?" my father asked. "Killing *who*?"

"Does it really matter, Frank? Can you *do* something?"

He went outside into the dusk and found the white-gas stove facedown in the dirt. At the edge of the campsite, a bobcat was tensed above our roast, though we didn't know it was a bobcat yet. It was the doctors who told us that. Doctors in that part of the country could identify the shrieking.

"Ohgodohgodohgod," my father said. He was not a strong man, not a brave man, but he stood there, barefoot in the grass of our campsite, turning himself into a wall between that wild thing and me. He kept his eyes on the bobcat and reached back to the collapsible table where he'd done the dinner prep, grabbing the kitchen knife by its blade and holding it out in front of him. He squeezed it tightly enough to sever his finger above the knuckle, so cleanly that it took several seconds before the blood and pain arrived—and then he started screaming.

The bobcat arched its back and its hair stood in a ridge. It made that shrieking sound again. My father was a wall, sure, but the cat was a wall with teeth.

It hissed much like the roast had done. I was close enough to smell its breath, though I was still a foot away. I was banging a pot with a wooden spoon. We'd had a cat once, Blackie, when I was six. She'd been flattened by a car. *Isn't it interesting,* I thought, clamoring up to the bobcat, *that this wild thing that eats rodents and grass has breath that smells like cat food. Just like Blackie.* I thought, *Maybe I'll be mauled.* I'd watched one of those wilderness programs with my father, and that was the word they'd used: *mauled.* It had a slightly spicy sound, and seemed to go nicely with all my father's cooking.

But I wasn't mauled. I got closer and closer, banging on my pot. Finally, I'd chased it off. The bobcat popped off of its position like it had been wound up on springs, and when it was good and gone, deep in the woods, my father said, "Christine!" like he'd only just noticed I'd come walking past his legs. I'd turned to see my mother, at the back of the tent, cradling the sleeping bag where I should have been—pressing it up against her chest—tranquilized with fear.

Self-Rated Affect Log, 4:23 PM
Joy: 3
Calm: 7
Pride: 2
Bashfulness: 1
Fear: ∅

As I'm being cranked up the Big Devil, I find that my thoughts turn toward Carl.

Carl wanted there to be more death-defying in our act. "Why do people go to amusement parks?" he'd asked me, when I told him we might experiment at *Bang For Your Buck*. "Not to *amuse* themselves, Christine. To feel like they're going to die. You build a coaster that can actually kill a man, you'll have them lining up around the Beltway. You'd make a *bundle* on that one."

Carl Feck, my love, or so I'm told. Dr. Blau was excited enough to bunch the sleeves of his lab coat in his fists. He'd said, "A love response is a very positive thing, Christine. The fear response lies latent in most love responses. There may be some part of you, right now, afraid he's going to die. That's good."

"Who said anything about love?" I'd said.

"You went out to dinner, right? You had fun? What else could it be?"

Beneath me, everything spreads. Though this is a mid-sized city, from above, most of what I see are the brown-gray nimbi of skeletal trees. I hadn't said we'd had fun. Carl and I, that is.

The cars ratchet up. If the coming drop proves unterrifying, we'll cross <u>Item 267</u>, *Veloxrotaphobia*, off the list. Along with the drop, Dr. Blau has chosen the Big Devil because of its design—a coaster built to simulate the wooden-style of the 1920s. Its ricketiness is said to produce a heightened expectation that the drop will not be caught by its construction—that the beams might break apart as we plummet head first toward the asphalt at 100 MPH. This, I understand, is the thrill: the fantasy that our brains will be splayed across the ground.

There's an old-timer in the seat next to mine, and her construction, too, looks less than reliable. She raises one arm into the air.

"Hold onto your purse, Sweetie," she says.

I have no purse. Ever since we crossed off <u>Item 103</u>, *Hobophobia*, Dr. Blau has thought it best to hold my pocket money.

I met Carl at a party while the Portable was strapped to my hips. We'd rigged it so that all the wires would come down on the inside of my shirt into a pouch clipped around my waist. The Portable is only about 85% reliable, but Dr. Blau says it's better than nothing, and that I have to start doing things out on my own again. He says that almost half of a natural fear response is generated from the alienation of being independent. In other words, he says, a free-fall skydive isn't relevant because of the possibility of chute malfunction, pancaking the diver in the field below, but because of the total disconnectedness—an independent soul suspended in nothing more than air.

"Then why parties?" I'd asked. "At a party, I'll be with people. I'll be interacting. I won't feel the disconnection of a fall."

"Just you wait," said Dr. Blau. "Besides. You're young. You should be out experimenting with pleasure."

It was about this time I began to think that maybe Dr. Blau was losing it a bit. Not *all* of his marbles, but every once in a while, a few of them would spill out of his brain-bag. He'd always rally, though, and gather them back in again. Then he was back to being Dr. Blau.

The party was hosted by a woman I'd known in high school. When I'd bumped into her at the Shop Rite, she'd said, "Christine! My god! You're here!" like I was a celebrity returned for a visit. "I'm having a party. Cute guys! How *are* you! Anyway, you have to come." Her name was Shirley, though in high school, they'd tormented her by calling her Laverne. The skin of her face was pulled back tight enough to widen her eyes in a permanent sort of way. She'd clutched me under my armpit.

"Okay," I'd said.

At the party, I'd spent most of my time near the cheese station. An orbicular woman was re-applying brie to her crackers in such a way as to make each application look like she'd just discovered the cheese wheels. "Oh my!" she'd say, "Brie!" and continue to spread it on. By her third visit, her voluble presence had quarantined the area, and I stood next to her unmolested by the partygoers.

Then Carl caught sight of my pouch as he was cutting up limes at the sink.

"Marsupial sighting," he said, pointing the tip of the knife at my stomach. One of the lime wedges skittered on the edge of the cutting board and fell to the floor. He kept the knife pointed at me as he got closer, smiling and making his lips wet with his tongue. When I described this to Dr. Blau, he said, "Well?" and I said, "Nothing. I was looking at the way his mustache has a gap right where the chute comes down between his nose and his lip. I was wondering if he was the kind of man to shave himself there." "Oh," said Dr. Blau. "Nothing from the knife, then." "Nothing," I said.

When he was close enough, Carl flipped the knife in the air and caught it so that he was holding the blade between his fingers. He tapped on The Portable with the handle. "Baby on board," he said.

"Careful," I said. "That's sensitive equipment."

"This is a party, Little Lady, not a camping trip. What the hell ya got in there?"

At this point in telling Dr. Blau the story, he'd scribbled furiously on his pad. When he scribbles like that, he makes sure to look up at me and nod his head every once in a while to let me know I'm still a person, and not just a piece of lab equipment, myself. Dr. Blau has a mustache, too, but it goes all the way across and is completely gray, and when he wants me to know I'm still a person, it quivers ever so slightly with concern. "Let me guess," he'd said, scribbling and looking up at me, making his mustache quiver. "You told him exactly what it was. You weren't afraid that he would belittle you or make you the center of attention at a party full of strangers, or even try to steal this very expensive device."

"Yes," I said. "That's exactly what I did. I said to him, 'This is a portable brain-monitoring device that measures my levels of fear, in spite of my damaged amygdalae.'"

"And how did he respond?"

"He said, 'What's an amygdalae?'"

In fact, I'd unzipped The Portable's pouch and shown him how the wires ran beneath my sweater, and how they were attached to my sides with adhesive pads that measured how much my body perspired. To do this, I had to lift up my shirt and show a lot of skin beneath my bra cups. Carl had said, "Whoa, Momma. I didn't know it was *that* kind of party," and looked around to see who else was smiling. But the two of us were alone in the corner of the room in such a way as to make it a private joke. Even the cheese-lady had gone away.

"Look," I said. "These were designed for social experiments." I showed him how the wires telescoped down to be almost as invisible as fishing line as they climbed the sides of my face behind my ears, and how they entered two extremely small holes that had been drilled into the base of my skull. When I lifted my hair, he could see the anti-bacterial tape that I can reapply, at this point, without looking in a mirror.

"Did it hurt?" he asked.

"I was under."

"So, let me get this straight. You're not afraid of *anything*?"

"I don't respond to those kinds of stimuli. At least, not the same way that you do."

"So, you've never been scared."

"Not in the way that you've been scared."

"*Ah!*" he said, flipping the knife into his fist and jabbing it just short of my eyeball. "*Ah! Ah! Ah!*"

Self-Rated Affect Log, 4:25 PM
Surprise: ∅
Anger: ∅
Shame: 3
Alertness: 9
Fear: ∅

As the Big Devil makes its final clicks upward on the parabola of its tracks, the wind rushes into the open collar of my jacket. The wind is cold, but I resist the urge to zip the jacket up. I want to feel the cold against my throat. What I've learned is that we are not always what we carry inside our bodies. For example, I am a woman in an amusement park, and not these twisted, sputtering nuclei that are housed inside my skull. The old-timer next to me flashes a gray-toothed grin. "That was child's play," she says, and I nod my head. This next one will be bigger.

"The clicking is scary, too, right?" I ask her. "People find the anticipation to be frightening?"

Her smile fades, and her eyes go bleary as she decides whether to pretend she hasn't heard me.

"I read up on it a little," I say. "It's the feeling that you can't get off, even if you want to?"

Free Association Memory Entry:
The Time Carl Said Holy Cow

"Holy cow," Carl said. "I mean really, holy cow. You have no idea what a coincidence this is. Guess what I do as a hobby."

"You pitch horseshoes," I said.

"No. Make a real guess." Then he said, "I'm an archer."

He took out his phone and started jabbing it with his thumb. "What's your number?" he asked. I gave it to him. In another second *my* phone started buzzing.

It said: Im a gddam archr n ill blw yr mind!!!

Carl stood there smiling.

"Like with a bow and arrow?" I asked.

"Exactly."

"Hmm," I said. I'd known a marksman as a girl. A faintly acidic rush came over me that may have been nostalgia. I thought to rate, but didn't.

"Do you get it?" he said.

"I think I do."

"Here." He went back to the kitchen counter and grabbed an uncut lime. "Take this." Then he turned to face the living room, which is where the rest of the party had all collected. "Excuse me everyone. Excuse me," he said. I saw how big Carl was because now he was standing fully beneath the kitchen light. He was like a lumberjack with those broad shoulders and stiff belly. His forearms were fat enough to swing a couple of axes at great northern trees. His jeans, though, still had the package-creases, as if wearing pants was special for this occasion. "Everyone just stay where you are," he said to the party.

"Don't move an inch. I'm going to my car to get my bow. Christine and I are going to perform a trick."

The party turned to look at me as I stood dumbly by the cheese station.

Laverne was sitting on the floor, propped up on some throw pillows. She'd been tilting her head back so that the group of men on the sofa could feed her segments of an orange, but Carl's announcement froze the hand of the feeder before he could lower the next one to her mouth.

Laverne looked up. Something like a feather had adhered to the corner of her lip.

"Not the bow, Carl," she said.

"Do not move," he said.

He'd intended to be out and back to his car so quickly that he didn't close the door. A fine mist of snow blew in. All the living room heads turned to look at me again, as though I'd been the one who'd caused the draft. The cheese station was once again a pariah's outpost.

"How do you know him, Shirley?" I asked.

Our conversation now was everyone's conversation, and I felt that ache in my throat I get when I've caught the attention of a group. Laverne's hair was swept back and fanned over the cushions so that she looked ready for a photo shoot. It was red hair, which matched her very red lips. She hadn't had red hair in high school. She hadn't had those milky shoulders, either, and I had the sudden sensation that my being there was the result of an uncanny coincidence—that she only *looked* like a girl I knew in high school named Shirley, and though she was not that girl, her name was Shirley, too. And I looked like a girl *she* knew in high school named Christine. But I was a different Christine. I felt I might indeed be in a house of strangers with The Portable strapped to my waist.

Isn't this interesting, I thought.

If I was experiencing any fear, an electrical pulse would have flashed across the gauge on my hips and blipped Dr. Blau's monitor all the way on Keswick Road, sending him tumbling from his late-night workbench, and tucking his pants into boots. If I was even close to having a fear response, he would be high-stepping it to his car through the snow, racing to pull me from this living room and back into the lab. But nothing like that happened. Instead, I stood at the center of the party under cockeyed lights and visions of doppelgangers, thinking, *Isn't this interesting.*

"You don't remember him?" Laverne said. "Oh, come on. Carl? *Carl?*" One of the orange-feeders bent his head to stare at her. "You remember Becker's cat?" Mr. Becker had been our high school principal. The sense of strangeness peeled away. Proof! He had brought his cat to school to take care of Schectman High's rat population. It was kind of a joke, meant to endear him to the student body.

"And then," Laverne said, "it turned out it hadn't been the cat at all. It was *Carl* killing all the rats. Remember? That's why everyone called him Pussy."

I did remember. *Further proof!* Pussy. He hadn't looked like such a tucked-in woodsman then. He hadn't looked like anything at all. He'd just been a name, Pussy, and when it was shouted in the hallways, there followed, always, the crash of a body into the metal of a locker. I remembered that sound, how it would clammer behind me and how the boys with glasses would flinch and the girls would hold their throats, and I would think, *Isn't this interesting.*

When Carl came back, there was snow on his shoulders. He was carrying a bow, the handle so shined with urethane that it glinted like glass beneath the lights. He rushed to me and I could feel the freezing outline of his body. He was like a sub-zero silhouette. That's how I think of him now.

Love?

Self-Rated Affect Log, 4:27 PM
Sensitivity to Light: 3
Alertness: 9
Fear: Ø

At the height of the coaster we pause, and I imagine that the boys and girls in the other cars, and even the old broad sitting next to me, are caught imagining a worst case scenario—that we'll stay teetering here until night brings down its cold, dark tedium, and the rescue workers have to show up with their rappelling gear. I imagine that, but I also imagine living three hundred feet up in the air again, spending my days regarding the breeze-ruffled feathers on the backs of all these gulls. When that kind of lightness is beneath you, how easy might it be to fly? The pause goes on forever. I am not immune to anticipation. I feel it acutely in my joints like an arthritic feels the weather. On the horizon below us, above the spreading gray nimbi of winter-nuded branches, I see the spreading gray nimbi of clouds of smoke from the most recent of the fires. Already, the mayor has banned the sale of glass bottles, due to their easy conversion to incendiary devices, but it's never such a simple thing as that. Like everything else, they make their way back into the system.

Now it comes: our car falls down its slope, then up-up-up, and down again. A balloon is being inflated in my stomach. I have to swallow just to keep it in. Maybe we're having fun. The woman beside me squeezes closed her mouth, I think, to keep her teeth from falling out. We do a corkscrew, and I hear her grunt. I am suddenly aware of the weakness of her organs, aware that the driver's license in my pocket identifies me as a donor.

As we pull into the station, I see the next group of patrons wide-eyed at the head of the line. Carl was right. Their smiles seem to want us to have died—for the rush of speed to have been thrilling enough to kill everyone on board.

"I'm alive!" I yell, and the carnie at the brake almost raises his head to acknowledge me.

The old broad stares straight into the back of the seat in front of us. Her gray hair has been ruffled and flattened like a piece of steel wool. "Never again," she says. "Never. Again."

We all stagger off. There are grandchildren waiting on the pavement below with devilish expressions. "She loved it," I say to them, and they look at me like I've reached out and pinched their little cheeks.

I don't see Dr. Blau, but I don't expect to see him. I head across the midway to a five-person water gun game. Wooden frogs stagger along sliding wooden waves toward a finish line. I pass a biker in a tank top with shoulders as hairy as a potbellied pig, and Dr. Blau leaps from behind the goldfish-toss holding plastic rats up to my face. He's testing for fauxmusophobia, Item 233: *Fear of Plastic Rats.*

"*Oogie woogie!*" he yells, but it doesn't work.

"Nothing," I say.

"Nothing on any of this? Zeroes across the board? Fascinating, Christine."

"How am I doing?"

"Oh," he says. "Just fine. *You're* hardly the issue."

I touch him on the shoulder, my own subtle reminder. It has been years, the two of us together. He looks into my eyes, unregistering, then finally makes his mustache quiver. "Sorry," he says. "Christine. You know you are *exactly* the issue."

"Thanks, Dr. Blau," I say.

When his phone rings, he tightens his face in such a way that I know it's P.J. Young.

"120 East North Avenue," Dr. Blau repeats into the receiver. "And this is happening now? Right now?"

Though he's no more than 130 pounds, and his beard is all but white, Dr. Blau's eyes are crisp, his nose as sharp as a shale formation. Sometimes I catch him regarding himself in the reflection of the lab windows, as if only now, after a lifetime, does he realize how handsome he must have been. Now that it's too late. Instead of handsome, he is kind. The fierceness of his sex is all but rubbed away.

"Let's go," he says. "This could be a good one."

"What's happening?"

"There's a fire in an artists' studio across town. Fire Department doesn't know about it yet. You have your affect-log?"

I look at him like he's asked me if I need to pee.

He raises his palm in the air.

"Okay, okay," he says. "In that case, away we go."

Carl rushed me around the apartment with his hands on my shoulders, but I ended up right back at the cheese station. He grabbed an uncut lime from the counter and held it above his head with two fingers in the manner of someone revealing a golden egg.

"Ladies and germs," he said, facing the partiers on the sofa. "I'd like to draw your attention to this lime. It has a diameter of no more than an inch and a half." He turned to show them all the truth of his statement, and as he did, the arrows rattled in the quiver slung across his back. The quiver was made of hand-tooled leather—the lopsided moons and stars of a hobbyist. "This young woman will be my assistant." He pointed the tip of the bow at the cheese station, which meant that the young woman he was talking about was me.

"Christine," I helped.

We hadn't been introduced.

"Christine!" he roared. "Come here, Christine. Christine is brave. Christine is fearless! What did you always want to be when you were a little girl, Christine? A star? Well, you're going to be a star tonight, Christine."

He took my shoulders and pinned them against the only blank wall. The others had framed pictures of Laverne and different handsome men standing in ski gear at the base of snowy slopes.

"What makes Christine different is that she is _actually_ not afraid. Am I right, Christine? Also, I notice that you have a very well proportioned and beautiful young woman's body. Even though you're, what, thirty-two, thirty-three? I bet if I lifted up the front of your shirt, I'd find a clean, flat stomach."

I nodded, obliging, and lifted my shirt to reveal a clean, flat stomach, along with the upper edge of The Portable, which was clean, white plastic with a flat tuning knob. I don't mind showing my stomach off to strangers, and I know that I'm physically fit. Because I am never afraid of becoming tired, it's exceedingly rare that I do; instead of sleeping, I run for miles and miles through the nighttime city streets, and I have seen my share of the horrible nighttime fires—orange glows on the horizon that I run toward but at which I never arrive. I'm often blocked with police tape and fire engines. It's only with Dr. Blau that I get in.

Carl rubbed the edge of The Portable and then touched the muscles in my stomach. He was like a blind man trying to memorize a face, and the party sat and watched him.

"Wonderful, Christine, wonderful," and though a few of the orange-feeders on the sofa cocked their heads, and Laverne, bereft of orange, seemed to sneer, I could tell that Carl had, for the moment, left his performance and was talking directly to me.

Then he turned and said, "An apple is easy. An apple has a wide and solid base. What we'll be using is this lime. It will not only require great marksmanship on my part, but great concentration and balance from Christine."

He took the lime in the fingers of both his hands and placed it very carefully atop my head. The bristles of his chin scratched my nose, and I smelled a hint of pickling spices on his breath.

"Be very still, Christine."

I held my head stiffly which did a strange thing to my peripheral vision. It made the orange-feeders on the sofa look like brightly colored fish.

"Really, Carl," Laverne said. "You promised."

I clenched my buns and the lime stayed put. Carl nodded his football-sized head and picked up the bow from where he'd rested it on a stool. "Steady," he said. "Steady." The goldfish in the corner of my vision were treading water, their fins fluttering madly to keep themselves in place. Carl marched off ten paces without looking at me, striding his right foot out, and then his left foot up to meet it, like a man who'd studied the etiquette of dueling. It made his buns, too, look like footballs, and I saw that this boy they'd all called Pussy had grown up into a linebacker. He could have crushed anyone at that party, and none of us in our wildest dreams could have stopped him.

Also, no one else was armed.

He turned to face me and his hand went behind his head and in one fluid motion retrieved an arrow from his quiver. He held the bow up and nocked the arrow, pulling it back and leveling it with my head. I waited for my amygdalae to send an electrical pulse to the wires and travel through the holes in the back of my head, down behind my ears, registering with the sweat-monitoring suction cups on my sides, and then into The Portable's translation chip, alerting Dr. Blau, and alerting me, with a slight heat in the filaments of the gel solution, that, at any moment, I might be experiencing something close.

But instead, all I thought was *This is going to be interesting.*

There was no heat from the filaments in the gel solution. The tip of the arrow caught the strangely angled lighting and seemed to drip with silver, but then refocused to look like a freshly sharpened pencil tip. I tightened the winch of muscle between my shoulder-blades, forcing my spine to stiffen, and the lime stayed where it was.

I opened my eyes wide as the point of the arrow traveled at my face and then disappeared into the target above my head.

"Ladies and germs!" Carl threw his hands over his head and the bow clattered into an inert ceiling fan. I looked up and saw the arrow's feathers, which looked to have been hand-plucked from the backside of a zebra finch. "Now, again," Carl said, "with my eyes *closed!*"

"Carl!" Laverne fumed, as if he were a misbehaving child. "*No.*"

The orange-feeders looked at each other, pursing their lips and raising their eyebrows.

I stepped away from the wall in the way I used to at the doctor's office, the arrow marking off my height at 5'6". I'd maxed out in the seventh grade. "Christine, this is only a tiny needle," the doctor would say. "Only a prick. Don't be afraid." "What?" I would say, and he would say it again, as if I hadn't heard. "What do you even *mean?*" I would say, and he would purse his mouth and raise his eyebrows like the orange-feeders were doing then.

"Wait, this will be better," Carl said. He was already pushing my shoulders back against the wall, pulling out the arrow with a jerk that pinned his armpit to my nose.

I smelled his moist, foresty smell—the funk of ferns pushing through dead leaves at the rotten start of spring. "If you liked that," he said, ignoring me where I stood, "this next one will blow you away."

"*No.*" Laverne's voice had lost all possibility of play, canceling the twinkle of Carl's showmanship. "Carl, no. You're done, I'm afraid. Once you put a hole in my wall, your night with me is finished. Are you drunk?" He wasn't drunk. "I don't even think you're drunk. But you're done. You have to get out of here." The orange-feeders didn't look so docile then. They edged up on the sofa and put down their citrus. I could see the muscles in their legs flex through their tight-fitting slacks. Suddenly, they looked like a group of bouncers being rallied for a fight. Carl can be fearless in his own right, but that is either bravery or foolishness, not chemical, and so it has its limits.

"Okay, okay," he said. "I'm not being impolite. My hostess says stop, I stop. Shirley, call off your dogs, huh? I'll be good. Look." He brushed me aside with a paw and stuck a meaty finger in the hole his arrow had made. "I'll be back tomorrow to patch it up. Bright and early. I'll make coffee. I'll make toast. I'll make pleasant conversation while you're sitting on the can."

"You absolutely will not. Just leave. Both of you. Christine, I'm awfully sorry I ever bumped into you. Serves me right for being the type of person to recognize a person after all these years. It was a compliment, and I take it back." By the end of her speech, she was standing with her own finger pointed at the door.

I left with Carl, out onto the snowy porch. He clutched my shoulders down the stairs, and though now I see that he was bracing his weight against mine to keep himself from falling, then I thought he was helping me on the ice.

That maybe he was sweet.

The art studio looks like one of those old brick sweat-shops, and the fire flickers up and down out of its windows. Yet there's something unassuming about it all, as if the flames were nothing more than orange windsocks, blowing in a breeze. Traffic is moving by. Down the street, music escapes from a restaurant as a couple of smokers go back inside.

"Any *people*?" I ask.

"I don't know," says Dr. Blau. "All P.J. Young could give me was the location. He got the call from some kid on a bike. He'll sit on it while you're inside. Good old P.J. Young."

He hands over the lump hammer, and I walk to the entrance and bust down the door. It's airy inside, a plywood stage painted black, a velvet curtain bunched on a wire overhead. I look for the stairs, but they're burning, full of smoke as thick as wool.

There's an elevator behind the stage, and the doors slide open easily on their tracks. Inside, it's just the shaft with cables going up. Wisps of smoke float down to me.

"I'm going up," I say, but more to myself than Dr. Blau. The cables are braided steel, as thick around as the handles of baseball bats, greasy on my palms. "Up," I say. "Going up, up, up."

Getting off the ground is the hardest part, but once I have my legs wrapped around the cables, and the tops of my feet are hooked, I slide one arm up and shinny my body to meet it. Arm over arm. The cables dig deep into my palm-flesh. My shoulders start to ache.

At the top of the shaft, I belly onto the wood of the second floor. It's covered in dust, and beneath the dust is spattered paint. On the other side of the room, a pyramid of cans glistens behind the flames. Paint thinner, maybe. Above it, the EXIT sign has melted so that the plastic letters look to bleed. I see the chasm of the stairwell, red hot up here—too hot even for smoke. Twenty feet overhead, the exposed beams are traced with shoelace-flames.

In front of me are puppets, easily twelve feet tall, even posed as they are in seated positions, stacked like office chairs. They're made of either papier-mâché or concrete, painted in the style of the Day of the Dead. Swirls of skeletal color, paisley cheekbones, arms and fingers bedizened with stars. Their shoulders and elbows are jointed, and the wires connecting them are bunched overhead in spools that look like fishing reels. A puppeteer, hidden in the rafters, might have made these giants dance.

I crawl over to save one from its fate, and am relieved to find it's as light as a piñata. It's clumsy, though. I have to stand and get it on my hip. The flames are concentrated at the far egress, so I feel I can take my time. Still, at the elevator shaft, I'm faced with a decision. Do I dally and look for rope to tie the giant puppet to my back? Or do I simply let it fall?

I let it fall—and its lightness serves it well. It bangs its head against the wall, but lands without much damage.

I get the next one, and the next, before I start to cough. Maybe I'm being overly ambitious. I feel lightheaded and have to sit down.

When my brain has cleared, I take the log out from my pocket.

Self-Rated Affect Log, 4:55 PM
Awareness of Possibility of Death by Smoke Inhalation: 9
Euphoria: 7
Awareness of Arms and Legs: 6
Fear: ∅

I grab the next puppet by its ankle and drag it to the shaft on my hands and knees. It falls like a feather on the pile. Or maybe I've simply stopped being able to hear the sound of its crash. The fire is roaring now, so maybe it's gotten closer. I run my fingers along the floor to feel the splinters.

I feel the splinters.

Self-Rated Affect Log, 5:05 PM
Pain: 7
Euphoria: 3
Shallowness of Breath: 9
Fear: ∅

Behind the last giant puppet, I find a lady. She's young, as young as me, sleeping, or probably unconscious from the smoke. She's sitting in a pile of ashes in a way that looks like a rocket has blasted off, leaving only her behind. Her hand is all burnt up.

I watch her chest rise and fall, and then I yell, "I've got a live one!" in the direction of the shaft.

I take her under her arms and drag her like a bag of dirt. At the shaft, I hesitate . . . at least the landing will be soft, with all that papier-mâché. But no. I have to get her on my back, somehow—I have to get those droopy arms to hang on tight.

"I was only lighting a cigarette," she murmurs.

"What?" I say, startled by the evidence that she's not actually a puppet, herself.

She says, "One thing burns another," and I'm seized by the urge to hug her close, not to save her, but to tell her that *I know*. One thing burns another. It all happens so fast.

Instead, I hold out my hand and turn my face so that she can see the scar along my hairline. "From when I was a kid," I say, tracing it with my finger. "I liked to play with matches, too. That heat. I know you know. Then everything's out of control."

"Get me out here, willya?" she says.

"Okay," I say, "but you'll have to hold on tight."

I go hand over hand back down and get her out and leaning up against the building just as the roof cracks open and collapses. Sparks explode into the sky.

"Let me see your pupils," says Dr. Blau.

Item 63, Bufonophobia: *Fear of Toads*

Dr. Blau and I stood in front of a Plexiglas door. They'd made me wear a hospital gown, booties on top of my boots, and one of those antibacterial shower caps. Michelle, the zookeeper, was nice. She looked at me and frowned in a playful way. She said, "I know. It feels ridiculous. But we have to make you wear it." She looked down and pressed her chin into her neck as if to coax me into better spirits. But when she looked back up, I saw there were tears in her eyes. "It's this Chytrid fungus," she said. "It's just so awful. When I think about," she snuffled, choking up, "extinction. Excuse me. Well."

She opened up the air-lock and let me walk right in. It was hot and wet in there, well over a hundred degrees, and when I looked out of the front display, the two of them—she and Dr. Blau—both waved.

Then they left, through the exit to the snake cages, leaving me locked inside, alone.

It was humid enough to make the wispy hairs at my forehead begin to curl. My boots were for hiking, as instructed. The exhibit was dominated by a puddled rock face—a moonscape, but one that breathed with life. Bromeliads perched in bunches of pink and orange and green. Purple orchids, their stems supported in wire, epiphytes that gripped the netting on the walls. From miniature crevasses, there was peperomia—I'd had one as a child. Seeing it there reminded me: everything, even in this suffocating dampness, had the capacity to burn. Plants with needle-sharp spikes—their mottled flowers just as barbed, ready to rip into anything that moved. Though nothing moved. Nothing moved but me. The toads sat, oblivious, underfoot. They were everywhere, animate, but only just, spread out like cow pies. When I touched one with my toe, it hopped like hopping was a tiresome thing to do.

I had an hour, and so I sat on a rock and watched. Some of them were as big as catchers' mitts. Some were freckled, some were marbled, and some had goose-pimpled skin. Some looked dressed in army-issue jungle camo, some in desert camo—some camouflaged to blend with a crate of tangerines.

Next to FEAR, I wrote a Ø. I crossed <u>Item 63</u> off the list. Maybe I napped. I don't remember. Time passed along in a haze. My affection for the toads did not diminish; nor did it grow.

After an hour, Michelle, the zookeeper, came in to let me out.

Carl has a little Honda coupe that forces him to bend his body into uncomfortable positions. That night—though he'd been extremely careful with his bow and quiver, positioning them just so on the flannel sheet he'd spread out in the trunk—he crammed himself behind the wheel like a depressed contortionist.

"C'mon," he said to me. "Shirley's crazy anyway. She paid for all those dudes to come."

We drove down the snowy roads at breakneck speed, Carl swerving and skidding through the gray slush that occasionally sparkled as it arced above the windshield. Every once in a while, a streetlight bore its green globe into the pinking sky. Carl didn't ask me where I lived; instead, he pulled up to his apartment building—one of the tenement-looking blocks of concrete with a shared iron railing—and said, "One rule: shoes off. It's not just the snow you're tracking in. My neighbors have dogs. I don't want this place smelling like a kennel," as though I'd been begging him to come inside.

It was there that I saw what being called Pussy for so long had done to him. It had blanked him out completely. Blank walls, blank shelves, a refrigerator door without any magnets. There was an army duffel in the corner and an umbrella stand for his archery equipment. A bedroll on the floor.

"You can lie down there," he said, pointing to the bedroll, pulling his shirt out of his pants and letting his belly breathe.

I lay down on the bedroll. The Portable was still attached, as it was every time we ran a late-night experiment and Dr. Blau had gone to bed. I used to need him for the delicate process of removing the upper wires from the holes in the back of my head, and so became accustomed to sleeping on my stomach, arms pressed to my sides and still, in the way of someone *feigning* sleep, so as not to press false readings into the equipment.

"Quit feigning," Carl said. "I've had that pulled before." But I hadn't been putting him on. In my condition, I can fall asleep on a hot rail if I have to. I have no fear of letting go into my subconscious. .

"If you want to leave," Carl said, "you can leave."

"I know," I said. But I didn't want to leave. My eyes were closed. His bedroll had that same damp rot I'd smelled on his body. It was not hard to imagine myself in the rain, sheltering in the hollow trunk of a tree.

When I rolled over and opened my eyes, Carl was standing over me, munching an Almond Joy. Gobs of coconut were sticking to his face.

"You're not afraid of this? Of being here?" he said, and I said, "No. Not that I can tell."

"What about the machine? How 'bout taking it off. It looks expensive. I can't be held responsible for any repairs. You should know that I'm between careers."

"No," I said again. "I mean, it *is* expensive, but you won't break it. It was designed by one of the scientists who worked on Alvin."

"The goddamn chipmunk?"

"The exploratory submarine."

"Oh," said Carl. He scratched his nose with the hair on the back of his hand until he'd turned it berry-red. "Another thing," he said. He turned from me and fiddled at his waist. "This one's big, and I'm not all that graceful with it yet. I haven't practiced on many women. What I'm saying is that this could hurt."

"Okay," I said.

"You're not afraid of pain, either? What kinda freaky shit is that?"

"I can experience pain," I said. "It's like a burning."

He turned from me and dropped his head, and I could see his shoulders making little tremors. I couldn't see his hands. "Unnnh," he groaned. His elbows flexed out to the sides, and he tipped his body forward. "Unnnh."

It's unpleasant," I said, "the burning sensation, but there's so much in the world that's unpleasant. It doesn't all make you afraid. Isn't that confusing? That's one thing my condition doesn't allow me to understand."

"Achh," he said. Then, "Oooh, okay." The backs of his ears had become as red as the tip of his nose.

"Nails scraping a chalkboard, for instance," I said. "That's unpleasant. The touch of sandpaper. Zucchini," I said, "when overcooked. Unpleasant. But no one is *afraid* of those things."

"Ha-ha-ha!" said Carl, not laughing, but exhaling in little bursts.

"When I was a kid," I said, drifting off, "I had this thing about sitting in front of the wood-burning stove, all bundled up. It was like being unborn again. One day, I got fixated on the corner of that stove. I stared at it all morning. I knew it was hot, but I stood up and grabbed it anyway, until my palm was singed and the blood was bubbling. My mother was visiting a neighbor down the street, but she came running. She said she could smell it all the way across the yards. I'd passed out, but the skin got sticky and held me standing there. After the hospital, my dad had the stove removed. Then our house was always cold. I begged him to bring it back, but he said that was enough of that. I was six years old, but I couldn't understand. I *begged* him. Please, Daddy, I said. I'm not scared. I thought I was telling him I wouldn't touch it anymore. I'd confused fear with action, which lasted for quite some time."

Carl was still turned away from me, his shoulders vibrating as he worked his hands.

"*Carl!*" I tried to whisper, but it came out as a bark.

He turned to me. "Yeah?" he said. "What?"

In one hand, he held a triangular piece of metal that flashed like a mirror in the sun. In the other hand, a file.

"It's a broadhead," he said. "Gimme another second. I've almost got it right."

He tipped his head again and made his shoulders shake, dragging the file across the arrowhead with such speed that I readied myself for sparks. Even a barren apartment like that one had the potential to go up in flames, and I imagined having to drag him out by his armpits. It's the big guys who suck up every last bit of oxygen, and then inhale the smoke.

"Okay," he said, touching the tip to his finger so that a tiny bubble of blood appeared. "Any sharper and this thing would be illegal." He looked at me ready for a smile. I gave him one. He said, "Not that it's exactly legal *now.*"

He walked over to me, holding the arrowhead up to his eye like he was inspecting the karats of a diamond. I sat up on my elbows.

"No, no," Carl said. "Lie back down. Go on. Take your pants off."

I slid my pants around my ankles so that the skin on my thighs tightened in the cool apartment air.

Carl knelt down between my legs, and his knees knocked the hardwood floor beneath the bedroll. He ran his palm up my thigh, around my panties, caressing the bottom of The Portable. What do I remember? His fingers—like the bulbous ends of unwashed carrots. "Now hold still," he said, hovering the tip of the arrowhead above my flesh. "This is where you need to focus. If you're going to perform with me, you can't be afraid of this."

"I'm not afraid," I said.

"Unbelievable." He loomed over me, grinning. "What a find."

Then he began to trace the outlines of my kneecaps with the tip of the arrowhead. He went around and around in circles, exceedingly close to my skin.

"If you flinch here," he said, "you'll definitely flinch in front of a crowd. Flinching is the enemy, Christine."

I didn't flinch. He traced up and down my thighs, along my panty-lines, and at the skin beneath the Portable.

At my belly button, he slipped.

"Oops," he said.

I looked down and saw a thin red line. In a moment's time, the blood began to drip and smear.

"Are you hurt?" he said.

I cringed.

"*Are* you?"

"It's okay," I said. "It burns a little. You know? Like time isn't moving."

I looked at him, hoping we'd understand each other now.

"That's the way it is with me," I said. "Like it doesn't matter if I'm going backwards or forwards."

He looked at me a little funny.

"Carl?" I asked, but then he looked away.

Free Association Memory Entry:
The Time I Went To Camp, On A Lake, In The Mountains

I was thirteen when they sent me off to camp. Who knows how they found it. I guess parents talk to other parents. It was on a lake, in the mountains. I remember waking up to fog and dewy grass. Cold mornings. They packed me with clothes for the tropics and the first night there I had to spend thirty bucks at the canteen for a sweatshirt. There were boys there, too, all the freaks of the world. Some of them had no ability to trust. Some could not be surprised. A boy named Paul could only feel self-confident. There was an awe-less girl, and her remorseless sister. We played soccer and had swimming lessons in the lake. There was a rope swing we weren't allowed to use, and an arts and crafts room that we were. I made at least a dozen lanyards—butterfly and zipper stitch, and an almost-Chinese Staircase. Many of the campers became great friends, but on the final night, when they played the slideshow on a big white sheet, only half of them were crying. There were many still incapable of tears.

In one of the fields, there was a trapeze. A real one, thirty feet high, strung up like a cat's cradle: nets and guy-lines stuck into the ground with stakes, the ladder only half as wide as me.

I signed up for lessons. An instructor named Big Ron showed me that my hands on the bar could be a hinge, that I could flap my body like a gate. At first I was just content to swing. I'd feel that great falling feeling and be caught by the rigging of the ropes and the metal fasteners of my harness. I'd swish down so close that my feet almost dragged on the safety net, and then be rocketed up with momentum, finishing that last thrill of the lift, up to the platform on the other side.

"A smile," Big Ron would say. "Think of your path as a smile," and then he'd smile, too, a big one—bright dentures as straight as bathroom tiles.

On the trapeze, the wind whipped past my ears. Glorious wind! I loved it then, and knew it *needed* me. On the ground, the air was still, but when I rushed along the arc of those ropes, it existed in great deafening ribbons through my hair.

"What are you, eighty pounds?" Big Ron would ask me. "And you're flexible. That's *good*. When I was traveling, we were always looking for the eighty-pounders. Eighty-pounders are the circus gems."

"You traveled?" I asked him.

"Did I travel, she asks. Did *I travel?*" Big Ron would lift his head and look around for an adult. "Yeah," he'd say to me, not finding one. "You could say I traveled. I went just about everywhere in my circus days."

Big Ron taught me tricks. We'd strategize between my classes, eating ice-pops from the snack bar. He'd have a pen and paper, and sketch out one-knee hangs and forward-overs. I got good enough where other kids would come and watch. They'd skip their basketball and tennis lessons to sit up on the hill. *Hup hup*, Big Ron would yell, and I'd go for something wild, and maybe slip and be caught by the pulleys and ropes and come down herky-jerky.

I suppose that it was scary. The littlest kids on the hill would yelp, though I imagined they yelped out of respect for the difficulty of my tricks. *The Terrifieds,* Big Ron would call them.

"Listen to the Terrifieds," he'd say. "Listen to them, Fearless."

Big Ron would call me Fearless like that was my given name.

"Come on now, Fearless. *Hup-hup.*" He'd tug on the rope that was connected to my harness. "Legs up. *Legs up!*" And my legs would go up, through the space between my arms, over the bar, and I'd stay tucked there like a bug. "Hands off!" Big Ron would shout, and out would shoot my hands as I executed a perfect knee-hang. Even with the wind filling my open mouth, with my hair slapping at my cheeks, I could hear the Terrifieds down there whimpering.

If Barnum and Bailey had set Big Ron out to pasture, it hadn't made him bitter. He'd take me under his massive muscled arm at lunch and say, "Fearless, you're the reason why I'm still in this crazy game." He was in his fifties, but stalked the campgrounds in neon spandex that showed the currents of the muscles in his legs—his wide, bare chest as hairless and spotted as banana skin.

By the end of the summer, I could do those one-knee-hangs and forward-overs without the safety harness.

The Unimpressed were unimpressed, but Sam, who could never *not* be astonished, was astonished. Poor Sam. He sat in the dining hall saying, "Pizza! I can't believe we're having *pizza!*"

"Your ideal audience," Big Ron would say. He spoke to me like a protégé. "Too bad," he'd say. "The modern crowd is more like *him.*" He was talking about Paul. Paul who sat on the hill and snarled. The Terrifieds were terrified of Paul.

"Pffft," he'd spit. "What's so amazing about that?"

In the dining hall, they sat him and Sam together, hoping for a counterbalance, to no avail.

"Mozzarella sticks!" Sam would cry. "They think of everything!" And Paul would lift his chin and say, "I am going to enjoy these mozzarella sticks more than you. My enjoyment will be of higher quality, more pure."

"More pure!" Sam would say. "Amazing!"

In the shower house, Paul shouted, "I am excellent at making myself clean." We could hear him all the way down by the pool. At soccer, he refused to play. Instead, he'd open a leather briefcase filled with stubby knives, and throw them at the trees. He predicted each time that a knife-tip would pierce a trunk. "This one will go straight in. This one will *kill* it," he'd say, only to hit it with the handle, to have the knife clatter uselessly to the ground. "This one," he'd say with the next, "will be absolutely *lethal*."

He got better. Much better. As I was doing layouts and double-saltos with Big Ron, Paul was sneaking into the pine forest behind the girls' cabins to throw his knives into our hanging laundry. He got to where he could aim through the holes of a two-piece bathing suit, and stick the knife-tip into a branch of a tree on the other side.

I know because he showed me.

"Christine," he'd said, grabbing me after lunch, when the rest of his bunkmates were practicing their card tricks. "I'm going to blow your mind." He took me into the woods and had me stand thirty feet back from his performance. He had my safety in mind. "You see that pinecone?" he'd say. "I'm going to take it right off that branch."

And he'd do it, too. One after another, until the horn sounded to tell us all to come down to the track.

Later, he grew bold. "I'm going to toss it as high as I can over my head, Christine. I'm going to be looking straight at you the whole time. You understand? I'm not going to look up at all. That's what makes this so impressive. I'm going to catch it by its handle without looking."

And again, he'd be true to his word.

In the woods, Paul would flex his muscles and smile. "One last time. Over the roof of the cabin. There are two counselors on the road. I know they're out there. I can *sense* them. One is eating an apple. I'm going to stick the tip right in."

Pretty soon he was hitting birds in flight. "I'm a hunter," he'd say. "I'm a warrior chief."

I let him take off my clothes with a knife in each of his hands. He did it with the frenzy of someone seeing naked flesh for the first time, *each time*, and so the warm steel would brush my arms, would brush my shoulders, would brush my hips as my pants went down.

"I am being incredibly careful," he'd say, and I'd say, "Don't be. Not on my account."

Once, when I was wearing a camisole, he grabbed the shirt from the bottom, and I lifted up my arms. My chest was still new to me then, but felt even more novel as it escaped that tight, stretchy fabric.

Paul began to sweat. A deep cave-dwelling part of his brain was caught off guard by the way my breasts sprung forth, while at the same time a much more recent neural maladjustment assured his total self-possession. I watched his face tighten, the ancient, reactive brain commingling with his modern, flattened one. A bubble of hope rose inside me and expressed itself in a smile.

Hope! Hope that our brains can change. "I am doing this correctly," Paul said, but only to steady himself. He shook his head, as if ignoring forceful voices. His hand slipped and the knife dragged softly across my skin.

"I did that as well as anybody could," he said. "Better than one hundred percent of most other people."

"It's okay," I said, dipping my finger down to blot where the blood was leaking.

"You're not hurt," he claimed. "Not badly."

It didn't burn then. Not yet.

He said, "You're grinning like an idiot."

"I can dance," I said. "I can go, like, absolutely crazy."

Paul and I were practicing again behind the cabins.

"No," he said. "Just hold still for now. For God's sake, Christine. I _told_ you. I have a method already in place. Have you heard of the Zen archer? Of course you haven't."

"No," I said. "I haven't."

"Well, don't bother looking it up _now_. If you really want to know, just pay attention to what I'm doing. The way I practice would put all those other archers to shame."

He took a knife in each of his hands and faced me. He closed his eyes and blew percussive breaths from out of his nostrils.

"Are you ready?" he asked. The crease above his eyebrows made him look hilarious with concentration. It must have been the way my father creased his brow as a child, and why as he aged, he had such comically expressive wrinkles. It got to the point where he could yell, "Run!" or "Save yourself!" and I'd think that he was joking.

"Yes," I replied. "I'm ready."

Paul opened his eyes, and the air in his chest seemed to leave him.

"_Christine_," he said, imploringly. "_Don't be._" I'd never heard him say _anything_ imploringly, and thought that maybe, at that moment, something inside of him had switched. He said, "If you're ready, it will look rehearsed. It's the spontaneity that makes it good."

"Okay," I said. "I'm not—"

And the knives flew from his hands and went between my legs and past my ear, sticking into the tree behind me.

"Good," he said. "That was better. I was perfect again. You see that? That's the difference. I don't practice to be perfect. I practice how many times I can be perfect in a row."

He stepped away and turned to face a sapling, unzipping his pants to pee.

There was a rustling to my left, and I saw Roger, the compulsive mimic, hiding behind an oak. I liked Roger. In spite of his condition, he was kind; his face would twist up painfully when his mimicking went too far. It was clear that everything was beyond his control. Once, when the camp director split his pants, Roger spent a week stealing from the eight-year-olds' laundry so that he could do the same. There he was at every meal, waddling to the front of the dining hall, bending over to pop a seam. The whole camp would roar with laughter, but I could hear him whimpering, "Sorry, sorry," at the camp director, until each time he performed it he was crying, and then sobbing, until the nurse decided he should eat in the infirmary, instead.

Paul had his back turned, and a healthy stream going. He didn't turn around as Roger tiptoed toward the briefcase full of knives. He took two in each hand and faced me, holding them clumsily by the handles so that they knocked together. I thought I saw him smirk—the grimace of a troublemaker—but no, his eyes were doing a kind of shudder, as if trapped inside his face. Roger—the *real* Roger, who was stuffed inside that body—was pleading for his arms and legs to stop.

But I smiled.

"It's okay," I said.

My voice in the quiet air had concealed the last of Paul's sputtering piss, so that neither Roger nor I heard him when he turned. Neither Roger nor I saw that, without zipping up, Paul was throwing himself forward the way a furious athlete might rush against a blocker— though instead of a blocker, it was Roger he was tackling.

They crumpled into a pile of arms and legs and knife blades, and I only had the gumption to break them apart because I wasn't afraid of the sight of bodily carnage.

Paul was strong for his age. He'd done countless pushups and dips at the edge of his bed.

It was good, I knew, that Roger had befriended the nurse.

Self-Rated Affect Log, 5:46 PM
Irritability: 3
Perception of Strength in Shoulders: 7
Sluggishness: 2
Fear: Ø

On the horizon to the east, the sky glows orange—but the phone is mute where it sits in the cup holder. Officer P.J. Young must be busy with other crimes.

I turn and look at Dr. Blau's wizened profile; he's older now than my father would have been, but doesn't look much older than when we met. We seem to be driving around in circles, hoping that something frightening will happen. He's talking to me, warning me against all the nighttime running I do, worried that amplifying the reserves of serotonin in my brain will make it even more unlikely for a fear response to register.

"And it gets your heart rate going," he's saying. "In the middle of an experiment, it makes it difficult to distinguish between fear and simple exertion." A more sedentary life, he's always told me, would be more helpful to the experiment.

Ahead, there are two gas stations, and Dr. Blau crosses a lane of traffic to pull into the more expensive one. He stops the car and stares at me, his notebook in his hand.

He knows this eats me up, and speculates that my thriftiness stems from a lack of fear that I will run out of the time to accumulate possessions. "If," he says, "you believe you'll live forever, then little by little, you can consume everything you want to. There's no rush. Whereas the average Joe has to buy it all at once. Or, at least, that's what it must feel like from the point of view of human history. Like there's a sale about to end."

"I don't believe I'll live forever," I say, but the statement doesn't faze him.

"Of course not, but you're not afraid of dying, either. That's basically the same."

The phone starts ringing as we pull back on the street, and Dr. Blau presses the button for the speaker.

"Blau," says Officer P.J. Young. "Listen, we've got another you might be interested in." He sounds tired. How many more fires before this city is nothing but a smoking bed of ash?

"Where?" I say.

"Antiques shop on Clearspring."

Dr. Blau can drive like mad for a scientist, and we fly down a bend in the road that runs along Herring Park Run, big naked sycamores up in the sky, light from the streetlamps touching only the lowest branches.

"I realize I'm driving fast," he says. "But I want us there in plenty of time. In that neighborhood there could be gawkers, and gawkers get the FD to show up faster."

"It's okay," I say.

"Of course it is." There's a bite in his voice, and I think he might believe that now I'm not being scared just to spite him.

"I'm afraid—" I start to say, and he pulls the emergency brake so hard that we go skidding across the lane.

He grabs for his notepad again. "*Describe it to me. What are your symptoms?* You're not pale. Your pupils aren't dilated. Can you feel your arms and legs? Try lifting them."

"I'm afraid," I say, "that things have ended between me and Carl."

"Oh," he says. He releases the brake and pulls us over to park on the side of the road. "I see. That's just a negative expression of compassion," he says. "We've been over that before."

"I know," I say.

Dr. Blau sighs. The scientific method, I can tell, is in some ways just about repeating yourself.

"So, you didn't *actually* have a fear response."

"No," I say. "I guess not in the way that you mean."

"Christine," he says. "We almost crashed."

"Yeah," I say. "I'm sorry."

"In this job . . . excitement . . . you know."

"Chicken II is dead," I say, just as the phone starts to ring.

He ignores me, and holds it to his ear. "Mmm," he says, getting the exact address. His face has slackened as he pulls back into traffic, and I'm concerned about his memory. These days, he tries to write things down, but so much can happen in the heat of an unpenned moment.

The phone rings, and he doesn't care about Chicken II. Just like that.

Maybe it's for the best.

We have to drive through the strip club district to get to Clearspring. Lake trout joints and check cashing and old neon tubes that flutter with pink and orange gasses. Bouncers sit on stools in bowler hats and ratty jeans. Dr. Blau looks straight ahead and keeps his mouth flexed tight. He's embarrassed by what goes on just behind those walls—to have me sitting right there beside him, with the dignity of my clothes. I want to wrap my arm around his shoulder and tell him it's alright, that I've long since figured out the *whys* and *what-fors* it takes to inhabit the various states of undress. I want to tell him that—in spite of the setback it implies—none of those *whys* and *what-fors* have ever scared me.

We exit onto Woodmount Avenue, where the discount liquor stores and churches are already looking dusky in the waning light. In the winter, the sidewalk freezes up so slick that walkers have to stick their arms out. Police lights flash around a corner, and paint the crumbling wall of an abandoned building.

We park behind a Chrysler with deeply tinted windows. There are brown weeds growing from a sewer grate, and the concrete blocks of sidewalk have buckled in uneven peaks. The Chrysler, I see, does not have tinted windows, after all. They're simply painted black.

The second story of 3301 is charred—the windows exploded, their edges as thin and burnt as a brick oven pizza. Officers in navy blue uniforms touch their shoulders to speak into their radios, and yellow police tape crosses out the entrance to the shop. Officer P.J. Young was wrong; we're not the first ones here. The door has been taken off its hinges, and so the lump hammer hangs, useless, in my belt.

"What's this all about?" says Dr. Blau. "Those windows should be flaming. Do you hear any screams, Christine?"

I don't hear any screams.

"Look me in the eyes," he says, taking out his notepad. "Follow my finger. How's your heartbeat?"

I tell him that my heartbeat is fine.

"Mine, too," he says, a bit mournfully. "Mine's fine, too."

"I can still go in," I say.

"Yes," he says. "Sure. You can still go in. You can go upstairs. At the very least, the floorboards will be compromised. You could very easily take a step and come crashing to your death. Yes, yes, Christine. Why don't you self-affect rate here, so we'll have a baseline to rate against."

I take out the log and record my affects. My annoyance is at a 5, my pity, a 4 and a half. My fear is still a Ø.

I walk up to the taped-off space where the door once was and inhale a big draught of smoky air. Depending on where you're standing, depending on if the wind is up, this whole city can smell like a campfire. There are times when I'm up in a flaming room, and the smoke is billowing around me, and I feel like I'm on a foggy mountaintop and everything around me is clean and pure. Then I'll fill my lungs, and fall down on my knees, and be dizzy from the coughing.

Upstairs, I know that the furniture will be burnt down to smoking sticks. Black strokes will have flayed the walls like someone testing spray paint. The floors will be okay. Even down here, I can tell the floors will hold me.

I pull up on the police tape like it's barbed wire, and start to duck beneath, before I'm stopped where I am, still straddling it.

Officer P.J. Young is running toward me, waving both his hands. A few of the other cops have tensed, their hands at their belts. One of them drops to a knee.

"Christine!" calls Officer P.J. Young. "Stop!"

Dr. Blau intercepts him like a principal who doesn't like running in the halls. "Young," he says. "She's under my supervision."

I lift my leg back from over the threshold and stand on the sidewalk hugging my arms against the cold.

"Dr. Blau," says Officer P.J. Young. He turns him around so that it's private from the other cops. "That's not how this works. Once the site's been extinguished, it's off limits."

"Who told you to extinguish it? I thought you contacted us before the call went out. There's no way FD got here faster than we did."

"It's not like that." I can see Officer P.J. Young straining to get him to understand—to somehow communicate by squeezing his shoulder in such a way that his buddies back there won't see. "You got beat to the punch this time, is all."

"But we've never lost to the fire department," I say. Without realizing it, I'm standing right beside them. I do this sometimes—move without realizing what I've done. I can travel great distances, and have before, in fact, moved clear across the country only to notice it later (in any *real* way, that is)—sitting on an iron beam above some distant city, and thinking, *How did I get here, of all places, from where I was before?* These days, it's Dr. Blau who keeps me grounded—Dr. Blau who keeps me realizing where I am.

"Not the fire department," says Officer P.J. Young. "This was another rescue. Another *rescuer*. Sorry, Christine. He must have got here right after I called you." His face is as wide and apologetic as a sympathy card. "Barletta . . . or something," he says.

"What'd he save?" I ask.

"Well," says P.J. Young, "the proprietor, for one. Got him just in time. He's over at Saint Luke's now. Let's see.

This is an antiques store. He pulled out a bunch of knick-knacks. Stuff like that."

Suddenly, I'm curious. "What kind of knickknacks?" I ask.

P.J. Young clears his throat, but rattles off the list so easily that I know he's been impressed—that he and his buddies have been marveling at the rescue. "A lot of old duck decoys and Mickey Mouse watches," he says. "Cast iron doorstops and one of those mounted deer heads. At least a dozen dinnerware sets, a couple fancy clocks. The old man had a dog in there. A German Shepherd all the way back in a closet. He went up and got him, too. That was the man's dying wish."

"Did he?"

"Die? No. Like I said, he's over at Saint Luke's."

"Pull the dog out, I mean."

"Oh. Yes. Turns out the dog was stuffed. That's how we found him. Walking through the flames with a stuffed dog under his arm."

"And this man," say Dr. Blau. "Barloney is his name?"

"*Hey, Williams,*" P.J. Young calls over his shoulder, and one of the cops raises his head. "*Barletta?*"

"What *about* Barletta?" Williams says. "Rocko Barletta?"

"Nothing," says Officer P.J. Young. His cheeks flare, red.

Williams must sense it, over there biting his tongue, and lobs a few more sentences our way like so many live grenades.

"Hey, Young," he calls to Officer P.J. Young. "Why're you asking about Barletta? You know it was Barletta again."

"*Again?*" says Dr. Blau, and I watch the muscles in P.J. Young's shoulders drop like they've been cut.

"Yeah, okay," he says. "This isn't the first time he's made a rescue."

"From a fire?" I ask.

"This guy, Barletta . . ." P.J. Young makes a sour face, as if he can't quite get the name to come cleanly off his tongue. "He's been rescuing people a lot. All over town. That coffee house fire on Seneca? He saved a hundred and fifty pounds of Arabica beans. Remember the blaze on Clay Street? That little pizzeria?"

"I've been there," I say, excitedly, but Dr. Blau shushes me with a look.

"They'd just gotten a shipment of pepperoni. Prime stuff, straight from Calabria, the owner told me."

"Calabria," I say.

"Yeah, and he saved the owner, too." He looks up at Dr. Blau as if to get permission to keep on talking. "Who knows, Christine? Maybe he read about you in the paper. Maybe you inspired him. Anyway, who can argue with what he's doing? Right here he even filled a bucket at the sink and saved most of the south-facing wall. You've done that before, haven't you, Christine? I know you have."

"A copycat!" says Dr. Blau.

P.J. Young shakes his head like he's sad to set him straight.

"No, Doc. A copycat impersonates. This guy is going bigger, one-upping you."

"What do you mean, one-upping?" says Dr. Blau.

"I mean, like, above and beyond. Christine, you pulled that eighty-three-year-old out of the rowhouse on Greenmount this morning, right?"

"Yeah," I say.

"An hour later, Barletta pulled an eighty-*four*-year-old out of a rowhouse at Waverly Place."

"Eighty-four-year-old," I whisper, and something in my stomach sinks. If I were to self-affect rate right now, my pride would register the hit.

"Last week, what'd you get from that house in Remington?"

I think back to the house in Remington. "A man, this little tabby cat, and a set of Coke cans from around the world."

"Yeah," says Officer P.J. Young. "And that's all fine. That's great, really it is, Christine. But that same day Barletta got a man, a *Siamese* cat, and a baseball card collection with a '36 DiMaggio in mint condition. I didn't have the heart to tell you."

Dr. Blau looks at the crack in the cement he's standing on—three lines that could be either a trident or the inside of a peace sign. I remember when I first started working with him, he showed me ink-blot patterns, and all I saw were flames.

P.J. Young says, "Over on Hartford Road, Christine, you got that woman, her two kids, and her saltwater aquarium? You remember? You saved all those expensive fish. Just two doors down, Barletta got a woman, her two kids, a saltwater aquarium, *and* the kids' Chilean au pair. Eighteen years old. Not a word of English."

"Not a word?" I say.

Dr. Blau stares deeper and deeper into that cement-crack.

Finally, he says. "I just can't believe this, Jenny."

Sometimes, I've been noticing, it's when Dr. Blau is staring deeper and deeper into something, that he calls me Jenny. It's a tic he has, along with blinking his eyes very rapidly, and scratching the back of his hand until it starts to bleed.

"Christine," I correct him gently.

Dr. Blau looks to P.J. Young. "Barletta, is it? I'd like to talk to this man. Christine, it might be good for you to talk with him, too. We can run some tests, have him affect-rate. A conversation between the two of you could be edifying. I'll need to get his information from you, Young."

"Ah," says Officer P.J. Young. "That's a no-can-do. The guy stays for the reports because he has to, but then he scrams. I'm telling you, it's weird. The other day, there was actually a news crew. Most people, heroic-types, they want to stick around for the news crew."

"Did you get an address?" asks Dr. Blau.

"Should have got his address. *Should* have." Officer P.J. Young rubs the back of his pen on his pad, but produces no address. "See Williams over there? That's his only job. His only job and he screws the pooch. Sorry, Doc."

Dr. Blau steps on the crack with both his feet as if to deny its presence; he's decided on something firm. "You'll hold him for us next time?"

Officer P.J. Young shakes his head. "No promises," he says.

"Delay him?"

"He doesn't like to stay."

"Give him an award or something? Check him for burns? I know you know how to stall. We just need to get him talking."

"If the man doesn't want to stay . . ."

Dr. Blau's whole body wilts like a lily, and I want to pick him up and dunk his legs in water. I don't know about all the men in his profession, but for him, the space between the cover of *Current Biology* and last place at a science fair is never very wide.

"If we have to find him, we'll find him," I say, but how do you find a single man in a mid-sized city when your only lead is flames? How can we ever stop looking, when everything always burns?

"Let's go back to the lab," I say. "We can run those new status tests."

"No problem," says Dr. Blau, though he says it very softly. "Sure. I'll take you back to the lab and kill you violently."

I put both hands in my pockets, and Officer P.J. Young turns to look away.

"It will be very painful at first," says Dr. Blau. "I'll use dental instruments to hook your skin and eyeballs. Then I'll let you bleed to death."

Now it's my turn to shake my head.

"I'll expose a good deal of your skeleton while you're still alive. You'll see your own bones before you die."

"Dr. Blau," I say.

"Oh, Christine," he says. "Play along. It's important that we simulate a death-experience. It will be death-*like*, at best."

"Oh," I say.

"I have the tools. The tools alone could be terrifying."

"Sure," I say. "A death-experience."

"Oh, hell. It won't work *now*. Now that I've gone and told you."

"Oh," I say again.

"Listen. I really *am* going to kill you. I'm going to cut you up and leave you on the floor for dead."

"Too late, Dr. Blau," I say.

"Of course," he says. "Of course you're right, Christine."

For the talent show, we signed up to do our act. Paul was very excited. "You've seen other knife throwers before, right?" he asked.

I hadn't, but I said I had.

"What we've been doing will blow all that away."

We'd also been practicing a dance. Even deeper in the woods, we'd found a bluff that lifted from the ground like the side of a barn. It was a wall of dirt and roots, and it crumbled when we touched it. Paul had a portable boombox, and he'd set it on the ground and turn it up to play _Bad_. Then I'd start to dance. Not like Michael Jackson, just wild, erratic movements. Headbanging was big a few years after that, but this was more bizarre. I jerked and convulsed. There was no predicting where my hands and legs might go. Paul would bop his head. He'd have on Bob Dylan-style sunglasses, even in the shadows of the trees. He'd pop the clips on his briefcase and pull out the knives, three in each hand, holding them by their tips between his knuckles. Then, casually, he'd turn his body, and face an audience of squirrels.

"Here I go," he'd say, bowing, but lifting his arms behind him so that the knives spread out like feathers. Then he'd spring upright, square his body, and one-two-three-four-five-six the knives would fly and cut between the spaces of my flailing body, sticking into the roots and dirt behind me.

But at the talent show sign-up sheet, all he wrote was "lip-sync."

"What lip-sync?" I whispered.

"I'm being smarter than them," he said. "You think they're going to let me throw a bunch of knives at you? Even knowing what they know about my incredible knife-throwing ability?"

The other performers were milling around backstage. The campers who I'd known as Samantha and Burt and Steven were suddenly shaking out the kinks in their legs, cracking their knuckles, running up and down scales on their guitars, and singing *Do-Re-Mi*'s like real performers.

I cracked my knuckles, too. I sensed that the air was thick with something, though I couldn't say what it was. I thought, *This is going to be interesting*. Paul stood beside me, holding his shoulders back. He was concentrating fiercely. I tested out a few spinning dance moves and untied my hair so it would whip and splay.

At the on-deck circle was a man in a sweater I'd never seen before. It was a hundred degrees backstage, but his skin was white and cool-looking. I watched him talk to Jimmy Saur. I watched him nod his head as he scribbled in a notepad. As he scribbled, he took little glances down at what he was writing, just to keep on track. The rest of the time he spent looking directly at Jimmy Saur.

Then he moved on down the line, from one pod of campers to the next as they approached the on-deck circle. They cracked their knuckles and stretched and sang their *Do-Re-Mi*'s until they got to him, and then they stopped and talked and hung their heads with the bashfulness that accompanies questioning from a strange adult.

As we got closer, I heard him say, "On a scale of one to ten, then, how nervous are you now? Uh-huh. Double-dutch? How many ropes? Uh-huh. A scale of one to ten.

One is the lowest. A six? Can you describe the way that feels?"

The act before us was a comedy team doing *Who's On First*. They'd been practicing in line, and now the words *When you sign up the first baseman, how does he sign his name* were stuck in my head. It cycled like a song, picking up speed.

Paul had closed his eyes—he was in his trance. We stepped up to the on-deck circle, and the man with the pad smiled like a restaurant host. But when he looked at me, his smile trembled, and then his whole body trembled.

"You're here," he said. "Jenny. My God."

"Christine," I corrected him. "My name is Christine Harmon."

For a moment, I imagined that whatever was shaking his body would also squeeze a rush of tears from his eyes, that maybe I should ditch this whole talent show thing and high-tail it to my bunk.

He stared at the ground, like a boy, at my shoes, which were golden.

Then he said, "Never mind," and recovered himself; the tremble was far behind him. He asked, "And what will you two be performing?"

"Lip-sync," said Paul, without opening his eyes. He rolled his shoulders and shook his head in a spasm of preparation.

The man looked at me again. Perhaps he was waiting for corroboration, waiting for me to say, "lip-sync," too, so that he could ascertain how a lip-sync made us feel.

"Actually," I said. "We're doing knife-throwing. Paul will be throwing knives at me while I dance."

"*Christine!*" Paul hissed.

"Fascinating," said the man. "And you trust him to throw the knives accurately?"

"I do."

"And," he said, turning to Paul. "You trust yourself to throw them just where you intend for them to go?"

"What do *you* think?"

The man flipped a page and scribbled on his pad. "How would you rank your level of confidence—ten being the highest?"

Paul opened his eyes and folded his arms across his chest. "I don't believe in that sort of ranking when I'm ranking myself," he said. "I mean, it's a ten, if you want to be simple about it, but you're putting me on the same scale as all the other knife throwers in the world. I am *more* confident than any of them. But what's more—and this is important—you're putting my confidence at the same level as the most confident *piano* player in this line. As the most confident *juggler*. The most confident ballerina. Of course, that's ridiculous."

"Uh-huh, uh-huh," the man scribbled. "And how about you?" he said to me. "This young man is obviously sure of *himself*, but how would you rate *your* confidence level in *him*? On a scale from one to ten?"

"Six," I said, and Paul clenched his jaw so hard I thought his teeth would break.

"Six leaves a possibility that he will miss. Are the knives very sharp?"

Paul opened his mouth just wide enough to mutter, "The knives are extremely sharp."

"So, if he misses, he could cut you."

"Yes," I said.

"And you're not nervous?"

"No."

The man scribbled on his pad. "Rate it," he said.

I thought about all the other knife throwers in the world. About all the other piano players and ballerinas, too.

"Zero," I said. "I'd rate my nervousness as not existing at all."

"Unease?"

"Zero."

"Apprehension?"

"Zero."

"Fear?"

"Ha," I said, because Paul had a way of rubbing off on me back then.

The man scribbled on his pad so fast that a forehead vein emerged. He smiled and crinkled the corners of his eyes in a way that said, "You're doing great"—a way I've come to love.

"Ms. Harmon," he said. "My name is Nathaniel Blau."

On stage I stood in front of a backdrop that the drama club had painted for an upcoming production of *Grease*. It was made of plywood—a jukebox with six vinyl records floating in the air. Six! Perfect. Paul had scouted in advance. I would dance in front of the records and he would stick a knife through each one's center. He placed the boombox in the middle of the stage and didn't say a word. He had on his Dylan glasses. The audience was quiet. Paul had been telling people he was going to display his talents in a way that would give them all the shivers. He pressed a button on the boombox and the music came pouring out.

I danced, throwing my hips in one direction, my head out in the other. I pointed to the sky and strutted along the footlights. I had until the first chorus before I would step in front of a record and really start going at it. As the song developed, Paul popped the clips of his briefcase. I shook my head and let my hair fly. From the corner of my eye, I saw him bowing to the audience, all six knife handles pointing skyward. He went pole-straight with concentration while I did the world's greatest impression of an inflamed nerve-ending. There was a brief, electric frisson as the knife flew through the tips of my outstretched hair and *thumped* into the plywood set behind me. I thought there'd be applause, but instead I was lifted off the ground. My hair was in my face but I could feel an arm tucked beneath my legs, feel the bounce of being run down the steps and off of the stage. *Because I'm bad, I'm bad, you know it, you know* became fainter and fainter, and the rustle and gasp of the audience disappeared. I was being carried out into the empty soccer field, and Big Ron's voice was floating above me, choked with wonder and with grief. "I can't let you do it," he sobbed, and cradled me—all eighty pounds of me—against his chest. "Can't you see that I'm in love with you, Christine?"

Self-Rated Affect Log, 6:22 PM
Despondence in the Face of Potential Scientific Failure: 4
Empathy for the Potential Failure of a Scientist: 9
Peacefulness: 6
Fear: ∅

The cops have packed it in and left us standing all alone, when we hear the sound of broken glass. Behind us, another *whoosh* of flame.

It must have been a rear window because across the street we see the facing pane with stenciled letters "Rare Antiques" is still intact. The flames are leaping up behind it.

"A second antique shop!" cries Dr. Blau. "Right behind us! What are the chances? Christine! Easy now," though he's the one who's hopping foot to foot. "Look me in the eyes. Follow my finger. How are your arms and legs? How's your heartbeat, Christine?"

We get the lump hammer from the car and bash the bottom door.

Dr. Blau steadies me by placing both hands on my shoulders. "Remember, Barletta saved all that junk. The watches and decoys and so forth."

"What about it?" I say.

"You've got to do it better. Barletta thinks he can one-up us? We'll one-up *him*."

"How does that—"

"Whatever he saved, we'll save better." Dr. Blau bends over as with cramp, and squeezes the crown of his head. "What else did he say? Doorstops and dinnerware sets. He saved the proprietor, too. And he came back for the dog."

"Stuffed dog," I say.

"So, if you could save a real one, that would be optimal. And try for the high-end merchandise. Not all that schlock. Go for the heavy stuff that's hard to lift. Bureaus. A baby grand if you happen to see one. A proprietor of higher quality, fat from his success. Passed out, preferably, so that you'll have to drag him."

"What if there's no one there?"

"Just try," says Dr. Blau.

He looks at me, imploringly.

"And rate," he says.

I do.

Self-Rated Affect Log, 6:27 PM
Annoyance: 7
Pity: 5
Gratitude: 5
Fear: Ø

I walk inside the bottom floor, and everything is chairs. Recliners and beanbags and thick-cushioned things made of leather-looking plastic. But the air is cool. These upstairs fires tend to stay upstairs. Even the set of wicker patio furniture looks un-kindling-like. I follow the signs with arrows. *More on 2nd Floor* the signs say.

Half way up, I get that feeling I sometimes get, and pull the log out of my pocket.

Self-Rated Affect Log, 6:31 PM
Nausea: 3
Dreaminess: 9
Desire to Be in the Sky: 10
Fear: Ø

There's a *pop-pop*-popping that brings me back, and around the corner I see the fire itself. A row of clear glass vases is crashing to the floor, the shelf beneath them burning.

There's a growl coming from somewhere, but I can't detect its source. The fire has danced strange circles in the carpet, lifting up walls of flame around hollow spaces, a maze of heat I follow. I curve around and—wouldn't you know it—a real live German Shepherd is tugging the shirt of a fat man on the ground. He's face-down, passed out from the smoke. The Shepherd has him by the sleeve, making growling noises as he tugs.

"Good boy," I whisper, venturing to reach my hand in his direction. When I touch his fur, he turns and snaps, and falls back baring teeth. "Okay, Sugar," I say. "Okay, Sweets. We're all just trying to help." I reach out again and my hand comes back bloody. He's taken a good chunk of my knuckle. "Come on, now," I say, a little sterner this time. "Get over here." I clap my hands and make a rough barking sound that works. He relents, and I hook my fingers beneath his collar and weave him through the flames. "I'll take care of your friend," I soothe. "Don't worry. Come on now, boy. I'll go back for him," and I swear I hear him whimper. At the stairwell, I crack him on the rump and he goes clattering down the stairs.

Back at his master, I kneel and give the man a slap across the cheek. He grunts. Smoke and flames are filling in the gap of the semicircle that surrounds us. "Come on," I say. "Let's go." I slap him again, hard enough to leave finger marks on his hot pink skin, but he doesn't so much as flutter his eyelids. I squeeze his nostrils shut and from his mouth comes a puff of air. I have to cover it with my hand until he turns his head and coughs, and his eyes snap open.

He looks at the flames overhead. "I didn't mean all the things I did," he says. And then, "What kind of sham is *this*? I've been to my confession."

"You're still in the land of the living," I say. "I need to use your shirt."

"My shirt?"

He's sweated through it, all the way.

"Yeah," I say, "take it off."

"Heh-heh," he says. "Land of the living. Right."

He wriggles out and hands it to me, dripping like a mop. I drape it down over a patch of fire and then another until a little section of the floor has been extinguished.

"Can you get to your feet?" I ask.

"Let me see," he says. "I'll try."

He swings his thighs around and gets himself to a sitting position. His body is clean and smooth and sectioned in folds of fat. "Can I get a hand?" he says. I lower down so he can use my arm. He grabs my wrist, my elbow, my shoulder. I'm forced to bend and push my face into the moist hock of his chest. Then we're standing, face to face, and he's steadying himself with a hand against me. "Okay," he says. "Whew. Okay. Let's get out of here."

I take him down the stairs, and it's only when we're outside, steam pouring off of his porcine body, that he turns and has a look behind him.

"My store!" he says, dropping his face into his hands.

"You don't have to worry about that," says Dr. Blau. "What do you have up there that's worth any money? Nice bureaus?"

"Yeah," the guy says. "Sure. There are bureaus."

"Christine?" Dr. Blau raises his eyebrows, and I go back up inside. This time, I hunt around the downstairs first, until I find a rug the color of batter, rolled up like a crepe. When I shake it open, a couple of dirty magazines fall out.

I haul it under my arm to the second floor and throw it like a fishing net atop the flames. I run across it to a patch of hardwood that isn't burning. When my eyes adjust, I see the plenitude of bureaus, and bend beneath a mahogany-looking one to get a grip. I hoist it up and get it balanced on my shoulder. But as I lift, a drawer slides open and smacks me in the face. I reach up to feel just where it got me. Am I bleeding? The flames are making everything look red. I push the drawer back in, and lift again, and I have to lean my hip to keep it back in place. A drawer at the bottom threatens, and I can almost feel it go.

I put the whole thing down so I can take a breath, and now the top of the bureau is burning. Little flames do a lambent dance on whatever solvent has been used to seal the wood. If I try again, I'll burn myself for sure. Still. I *want* to try. I want to bend and press my body against the drawers to keep them penned where they are inside. I want to feel it all go up in flames around me—for the wood to radiate that wonderful heat, to let it pass from the flames into my body. To be warm like that again.

Self-Rated Affect Log, 6:42 PM
Trembling: 9
Trembling due to Fear: Ø

The edge of the log-book page crisps and bursts into flame. I have to stamp it with my foot.

I'll leave the bureau where it is, but there's no way I'll be able to face Dr. Blau. He has such high expectations. I grab the rug and beat out a path toward the stairwell. Then I hold it over my head and walk down and out into the night.

"Christine?" I hear through the rug. "Christine, what's going on?"

I drop it and run. Something has pricked me, as sharply as a bee.

I run, though the city streets are icy, because I've learned how to run on icy city streets. I've learned how to run on icy streets in the nighttime, too; it's just like being balanced in the air. I've had all that practice just letting the wind take me and steady, steady, steady. Fifteen stories up, 300 feet up, up on top of a flagpole—a small gust, a medium gust, a gust that might set me loose and free. I brace myself. Patches of slick, black ice and buckled paving slabs . . . . It doesn't matter. Now I really fly.

I hear him shout, but distantly. "Christine?" His voice is fading.

Up ahead, I see the blue lights of the Beltzerseltzer Tower, that old relic. They've boarded up the bottom and are taking the rotating bottle off the top. In the doorway, there's a man bundled up, sleeping on a piece of cardboard. He's wearing at least three knit caps, one atop the other, a red beneath a blue beneath a hunter's orange, so that his head looks as big as Carl's.

I take the lump hammer from my belt.

"Don't—" is all he says, raising his hands in front of his face.

"What if I were to tell you that I've rescued the contents of three buildings from fires today? What would you say to that?"

He's got those watery eyes that melt me, skin so puckered and scratched that I can't tell if he has a mustache.

"I'd say you're doin' a lot better than me," he says. "You're a nice lady, I guess. But I say let 'em burn. None of 'em'll have me anyway."

I say, "How'd you like to sleep indoors tonight?"

"A night inside is a night with pride," he says.

I bash the door, and together we walk in amongst the cobwebs.

"Oh yeah," he says. "This'll do." He hunkers in a corner and tucks himself to sleep.

I take the stairs three at a time to the top of the tower. At the highest floor, I have to jump to catch the bottom rung of a half-ladder and climb up to the ceiling. I turn the hatch-wheel that opens to the roof. There's a catwalk around the base of the bottle, and the bottle's overhead. It's tilted, Earth-like on its axis, as long as a limousine. Back when it used to rotate, it would break down all the time. I remember. I got the call to fix it once, back when I wandered in the sky.

Now there are temporary supports made of plywood, boxing it in while they finish cutting the bolts that hold it to its post. I wrap my arm around the metal base and look out on the city. I can see right down into the ballpark;

they keep those banks of lights ablaze even though the field is empty and blue with tarps. Across the water, the aquarium slants blackly against a purple sky, varicose neon lights in the shape of waves, and blocks of dwarfish skyscrapers, just office buildings, really, their lights dull and amberish. The wind comes up and tugs my coat, tries to pull the lump hammer from my belt. I lean my head back and let it blow my hair. The wind is cold and wants to take me over the edge, but I hang on. Everything is ready to leap out and glide or flatten against the earth. Another gust swirls at my face, but instead of cooling me down, it seals up the fire inside. I can feel it rage around within me. The wind is in my nostrils. To smell it! To smell all those men I knew before. Sammy and Preston and Charles and Mike! All those men who worked with me on high, who took me in and were kind when they didn't have to be. I've given all that up to be back here with Dr. Blau.

"Christine!" I hear him call.

He's 300 feet beneath me, his head poking from the car. His hands are circled around his mouth.

"I'm fine," I call. "Everything's okay."

He's shouting something else, but the wind's too strong for me to make it out. It's only when it dies for a beat that I can hear him.

"Rate!" he's shouting. "Make sure you remember to rate!"

"For a performer such as myself," Carl used to say, "a few drinks in the audience is just about mandatory. It enhances the illusion of imminent death. People start to titter. They say, 'Carl Feck shot an olive off a woman's head from 50 yards away.' They say that, and the next thing you know I'm performing at Caesar's for a hundred grand a pull. Imagine that. Imagine the gear I could buy. I'd put you in sparkles, too, Christine. No good assistant doesn't sparkle."

The fact is, Carl never shot an olive off a woman's head . . . but he shot a kumquat, an alarm clock, a tri-fold wallet, a pillbox hat, and a watermelon—just as it started to roll—off of mine.

Back at the beginning, we would drive around through the snow at the end of each week, looking for apartment complexes with balconies that had people standing outside and smoking. Carl would park across three spaces in the lot and call up, "Party?" and they'd say, "Hell, yeah. Come on up." Among certain types, the fires had ushered in a fun-loving spirit. We were never denied a beer, a cup of punch, a bowl of creamy dip to cool our piquant chips. Then out would come Carl's quiver. Out would come his bow. Up from the coffee table would go the 5 x 7 framed photograph of our host on a Sunfish sailboat. Up would go a handkerchief, a pocket dictionary, a tennis shoe from beside the door. Up would go a houseplant, a sofa cushion, a hot, dripping candle. Up they went, on top of my head, and with his finely honed arrows, Carl stuck every one of them to the wall behind me.

In the early goings, there was general screaming and running about. I think I even saw some of the original orange-feeders (party-floaters, they must have been) flexing and waving angry fists. Often we fled, fishtailing through the snow until we heard the sirens. Then Carl would pull the car off on a side street and kill the engine, disappearing us into the pinks and yellows and watery greens of those winter nights. In the vestigial warmth of the heater he would teach me his particular brand of archery.

"A marksman has total control of his head at all times," I remember him saying, and I'd assumed he was talking about being "calm under pressure," a term Dr. Blau says doesn't apply to me. For me, he says, pressure is irrelevant. But then Carl would unwrap the cloth package he keeps his arrowheads in and pinch one between his thumb and finger.

"Take off your pants," he'd tell me again, and he'd run the tip up and down my naked thigh, so close I could feel the temperature of the steel without feeling the steel itself. I could feel his fingers trembling, too, and when he'd cut me (and eventually he'd always cut me—a laceration as thin as from a piece of paper) I'd say, "Was that part of the total control?" just to get him going.

But Carl couldn't take a ribbing. His face would darken in a scowl. He'd say, "God, Chris. I'm *practicing. God.*" And that would be the end of our conversation.

After a little while of our performing, we became a minor hit in town. It was said by some that a Friday night party wasn't a Friday night party if, on Saturday morning, you couldn't put a finger in a hole in your wall left by the arrow of Carl Feck.

Even Laverne called, begging us to come back.

"No way," Carl said. "A repeat performance? This early in the buzz? Makes zero sense."

Soon, our phones were vibrating with invitations.

"We heard you can shoot through a crowd," they'd say. "I have a hamster who needs to go, the little shit." Or Laverne, apologizing, "I was so drunk that night, I thought you were someone else. I thought you were the one going around stealing wallets out of jacket pockets in the bedroom."

"Tell them no," Carl said. "Let them wait. Let everything start to build."

"Or better yet," he said. "Tell them we're already booked at Caesar's."

And so we spent those nights in his apartment, ordering Chinese, sitting on his bedroll, eating and getting to know one another. He was the type of man who felt no barriers between the intimacies of our bodies, and would belch open-mouthed in front of me, or fart by lifting up a leg. I felt he had no secrets.

"When I was a freshman in high school—" I said to him, about to start a story.

"I remember you in high school," he said, closing his eyes to express the ecstasy of a mouthful of General Tso's.

Of course. He would have known me then. Part of my closeness to Carl must have come from shame. I can see that now. I wasn't part of the group that tormented him, but I'd done nothing to stop them, either. I'd let the sound of his body slamming into lockers enter my ears like any other sound, like sneakers on the freshly buffed laminate hallway, like gossip, like Mr. Soaperstein saying, "Can I have your attention? People? People?" A body slamming into lockers, and all it was was noise. I heard it as he removed my pants after our Chinese meals, as I adjusted The Portable against my hips, as he sharpened another arrowhead and traced my outlines with its tip. I'd done nothing to stop the blankness of that sound, the blankness that had spread into his mind, and leached into the way he lived—a way that hadn't allowed anything in the intervening years to stick.

But that was way back then.

"This was a class you weren't in," I said, not so sure it was true. "Precalculus with Ms. Sams."

"Ms. Sams was blind as a bat."

"Yeah," I said. "That's part of the story. You remember how Schectman was up on that hill?"

"So what?"

"So that classroom was on the backside of the building, and it was on the third floor, and because of the slope, the windows were like fifty feet off the ground. You remember? You could see all the way to the harbor from that side. So, one day Brad Adams and Isaiah Givens were messing around with a paper football."

"One day I'll kill those sadists," Carl said. His eyes were open. He lifted the fork from his bowl and squeezed the handle.

"Oh," I said, and thought about stopping the story, but Carl said, "Go on."

"Okay," I said. "Well," I said. "They were messing around, and one of the windows was opened up a crack, and when they flicked the paper football, it went through and got pulled back on a breeze and landed way down on the outside ledge."

"Uh huh."

"I was watching, so I saw it take a hook. Ms. Sams was writing equations on the board. I got out of my seat and opened the window all the way and lifted myself out. That ledge was probably only three inches wide, and I got up so that I had to press into the side of the building to keep from falling off. The paper football was really far down, maybe fifteen feet, but I did it. I went heel-toe all the way out there, bent down, and pinched it between my fingers. I wasn't scared. It was like I was walking fifteen feet on this floor right now, if this floor had a view of the harbor. I felt the breeze, and I saw all the dead grass beneath me, and I saw Jimmy Banks smoking a joint on the lacrosse field. And when I got back, I saw the looks on all their faces. All I'd done was walk very carefully, but it was like I'd been out on a real rescue mission, like I'd just climbed down from a mountain, and the paper football in my hand wasn't a paper football, it was something much more valuable and fragile, like a baby bird or something."

"So what?" Carl said. "I remember that. People talked about it for, like, one day."

"So, I thought I'd hit on a profession," I told him. "I was only fourteen, but I'd never really tried anything scary. I'd burned myself, sure, but I hadn't played chicken with my bike or anything. I was just starting to see that I was different, and I thought, well, I have good balance, and heights don't scare me. So I tested it out. I got up on the roof of our house and I tiptoed all around the gutters."

"Oh sure. Like they didn't break."

"I'm not as heavy as you," I said, and Carl frowned but kept on munching.

"I climbed the skinny ladder on the water tower as high up as I could, but they'd cut it off way before the bulge. Then I ran out of tall things. We live in a pretty low-lying town."

"No one wants to build a real skyscraper here. Where are all the jobs?"

"I had an idea to run away and join the circus. To be a tightrope walker. I'd always heard that people ran away to join the circus."

"You're a freak alright," Carl said. I was learning about his moods. Unlike other people, Carl was most pleasant when he let his hunger build. At 4:30, he was a dear. But after dinner, he was irascible, waiting for the pleasant feeling of fullness to pass, for the growl of his appetite to arrive again.

"So I ran away," I said. "I think I was the only runaway on the streets that still loved her parents. I had a dog then, Barkie, and I loved him too, but that's how much I wanted to walk the tightrope. I was willing to leave all that behind. But I found out that you can't run away and join the circus anymore. The circus is hard to find. I looked for days. I caught rides all the way to Paramus, but I couldn't find it anywhere. In the modern era, you've really got to plan that sort of thing."

Then there was the time I was almost shot to death when the parties were really swinging. We'd been to just about every kind imaginable; surprise ones, Western-themed, retirements, bridal bashes, murder mysteries, and a party for New Year's Eve. The one I'm remembering was a Mardi Gras kind of thing.

Carl had gotten good and lost on the way because the party was deep out into the country. It was so far out, in fact, that when it started snowing harder, Carl clutched the steering wheel and tilted his head up beneath the windshield as if he might see buckets of the stuff being poured on us just to spite him. "Jesus," he'd said. "What the hell do you think it takes to get a plow to come out here?" There were no streetlights, and everything was white, and at one point, he drove us clear out into a field. When he tried to reverse back to the road, the wheels just spun in place.

He sat there for a few minutes with his head against the wheel.

"This could be it," I said. I wanted to self-affect rate, but Carl had begun to hate it when I did, so instead I committed it all to memory. My happiness was a 7. My interest in seeing the look on Carl's face while he was possibly experiencing fear-symptoms was a 9, though my own fear was still at Ø.

I said, "This could be the way we die."

"Just shut up," he said, revving the engine so that the tires continued to spin.

I got out to push, but only rocked it back and forth a little.

"Put your whole body into it!" Carl shouted through the window. I was standing in eight inches of snow, and felt my toes becoming numb. All I had on were the ballerina slippers he'd picked out for the show, and my feet were soaking wet. Soon, I couldn't feel my fingers, either.

Finally, I got back inside and took the wheel, and Carl went behind. In the rear view mirror I could see him disappear behind me, maybe into the woods. I thought that he'd abandoned me, that maybe he was trying to hoof it back into the city. But then I saw the outline of his body getting bigger and bigger as he charged forward like a bear.

"Floor it!" he yelled, and he threw himself against the trunk. The car gurgled and rumbled out of its depression in the snow.

"Hooray!" I said, but when Carl took over driving, he did so stone-faced.

He cheered up at the party, though. Dr. Blau once told me that people perform their best—or even sometimes *beyond* their best—under extreme fear conditions. Or maybe it was the masks that got him going. All the ladies wore masks with brightly colored feathers, and the men wore black oval ones that hugged their faces in the style of the Lone Ranger.

Whatever it was, he put on a wonderful show.

By that point in our touring, we would bring our own bag of props. We had a Devo-esque hat on which I could balance water balloons the size of Crenshaw melons. They'd explode in ways we could augment with red and yellow food coloring. For that trick, we'd learned to elicit the help of our host to pass out ponchos. We also had two-liter soda bottles, shaken until they were hard as stone. An arrow piercing their plastic flesh would make a tremendous pop before the liquid geysered out. We had sponge cakes and strawberries and canisters of whipped cream, too. A few minutes later, I'd be covered in the evening's dessert.

But that night, Carl wasn't content with all the gimmicks.

Instead, he called upon his own frenzied talents, shooting from difficult angles, or shooting from off one leg. The house was a mansion, really, and it had one of those wide sloping staircases. Carl pranced up and down it, loosing one arrow after the next.

I'll admit that sometimes his ebullience got the best of him—and sometimes I had to help. I was like a mother holding out my arms in a giant O for a child to throw a ball through—jerking over at the last second to ensure his aim was true.

Afterward, when Carl was taking his bows, the crowd started filling back in. They'd been hugging the walls during the performance, which was not an unusual thing for an audience to do. Each time an arrow loosed, I could see out of the corner of my eye their collective flinching. *It was interesting*, I thought. The arrows weren't aimed at *them*. But imagining fear in other people was not unusual for me, either. I could understand it at its edges. It was more like *care* than fear. It was more like they all just wanted me to keep on living.

But after Carl took his bows, there remained only curiosity. The party-goers swarmed around me to touch my face and squeeze my shoulders. Maybe they were examining me for holes. Women ran their fingers through my hair, and men picked up objects from around the room—

vases and boxes of tissues and those compact stereo speakers—to see if they could balance them on my head.

Once, when it seemed like all the excitement had died down, one of them took a sofa cushion and placed it on my head like an oversized graduation cap. I stiffened up straight, and when he stepped away and the cushion stayed balanced where it was, there were a few *yay*s of approval. Letting the audience feel like they were involved in the act was an integral part of the show, and I searched the crowd for Carl, wanting him to see that I was playing along. He'd been harping on me during rehearsal to "get into it more," to at least "look like you're afraid you might be shot to death. A little showmanship, Christine." Balancing this sofa cushion would go a long way to show him I was trying.

But Carl had his back to me. He was standing between two gray-haired women in expensive-looking suits, his arms around their waists. His quiver of arrows wasn't on his back. *Isn't that interesting*, I thought. During a show like this, his quiver of arrows was always on his back. *And where is his bow?* I thought. *He never puts down his bow.*

Maybe it was the euphoria of being alive and dry and warm at a party after having spun his wheels out in a deserted snowy field. Maybe it was just the thrill of another successful show. Whatever it was, that night Carl did his flirting unarmed.

"Ladies and gentlemen," I heard from a voice that sounded remarkably like Carl's. At the opposite corner of the room, a man stood with the bow drawn back—an arrow pointed at the cushion on top of my head, just like Carl would have pointed it. The crowd around me spread away like his voice was a drop of soap—and they, a residue of oil. Carl had been big into using his *shalls* that evening, and so it sounded familiar, almost comforting, to hear this stranger announce, "I shall now shoot this cushion from atop my beautiful assistant's head." The man was wearing his Lone Ranger mask, so I couldn't see his face. But I could see that the dome of his head was alabaster in the lights, and that his chest and legs were thin. It was the kind of emaciated lank I'd seen before in certain vegetarian bachelors—and where his arms escaped a short-sleeved shirt, his elbows were as knobby as chicken bones. I was amazed he had the strength to draw the string back to his ear.

In less than the time it took for him to release his fingers (it had to be less, because the shot never came), Carl had covered the distance of the room. I watched him like I might watch footage of a sasquatch—a grainy streak of wild size that if I hadn't been standing right there, observing with my own two eyes, I'd say was done by trick photography.

The party was in an uproar. A few of the guests had collapsed and were fanning their faces. Carl was on top of the man, the bow and arrow sliding across the marble floor.

"Call someone!" someone called.

"Say something!" said someone else.

Carl reached his hands around the man's neck and squeezed, but he only squirted out of his grasp like a bar of soap.

The man was up and running—long, bungling strides, but fast, in no particular direction, then circling away from Carl as Carl gained his bearings.

Before anyone could stop him, he'd flung the front door open and gone zigzagging through the snow. I watched him disappear into the gray air until all I could see was his dull white head. And then his head disappeared with the rest of him, and there was nothing but fields and trees out there.

With the party murmuring behind me, Carl grabbed me by the waist. He was breathing hard into my ear, pulling me close against his side.

"Take a bow," he panted. "Just smile with me and bow. Say it with me: *It was all just part of the show.*"

I whispered: "It was all just part of the show."

We bowed. We bowed again.

The party went berserk.

Once, Carl and I broke into the lab. I'd assumed he wanted to steal scientific equipment to pawn, or find objects to shoot from off my head. There's a room to the side where Dr. Blau keeps the expensive stuff, and I worked hard to keep Carl from realizing it was there. The main area has just two stainless steel tables, a scale, and Chickens I and II. I thought, _How much damage can he really do?_

At least, I thought, he'd like to see Chickens I and II.

"What do you do to these?" he said. "Torture them? Make them wear lipstick and such?" He stuck his finger into one of the cages, and Chicken II screeched and clung to the rear bars, his white mane fluffed and shaking.

"Get your hands out of there," I said. "He'll bite a finger off."

Carl pulled his hand back and cradled it at his side, as if he'd already been attacked. Chickens I and II are three-year-old vervet monkeys with ashy coats and brown, liquescent eyes. Because we are afflicted by a similar condition, I think of them more closely than the distant genetic relatives they are.

"Rabid little pricks," Carl said. "Where's he keep the Bunsen burners? I have an idea to coat an arrow in gas, get a real high flame and shoot it right through. That way they can see it burning when it hits the wall. That'd be the proof of my aim, that it went through the flame where I wanted."

"Won't it burn down the house? Shooting flames into the wall?"

"Ever hear of an extinguisher? Thank God you weren't in charge of Copperfield's road crew, Christine. Your thinking is way too small."

Even then, Carl was getting on my nerves, but Dr. Blau told me it was a compelling aspect of couplehood to explore.

It'd be harder to convince me of that now.

"Let me show you something," I said.

From one of the drawers, I pulled a Pyrex case, as shallow as a cigar box. Inside were two ring-tailed corn snakes.

"Monkeys are hardwired to be scared of snakes," I said. "Normal ones would be screaming their heads off right now."

"Can I feed one a mouse or something?" Carl asked. "Do they constrict? I've always wanted to do this."

"No. Pay attention. Feeding is Dr. Blau's job and he's incredibly precise. Just watch."

I took the snakes from the Pyrex and draped them on my fingers.

"Here Chicken Chicken," I said, walking toward the monkey cages with my hands outstretched.

Chickens I and II came to the fronts of their cages and grabbed the bars like inmates. They commenced to jumping up and down.

"They're freaking out!" Carl said.

"No. They're just excited."

I let the snakes slither from my fingers onto Chickens I and II's upturned monkey palms. Once they had them, they scampered to their corners. They sat down and stroked the snakes on the tops of their heads. They made sweet, motherly clucking noises.

"Hmm," said Carl. "If there was a way to teach them how to balance a snake . . . . Will they stay in a coil? Can they be trained to do that? I have a feeling an audience would be inclined to applaud a snake killing. The whole Adam and Eve thing. What's the smallest object I've ever shot off of you, Christine? A quarter lime? Those snake heads are smaller than a quarter lime. But we could get bigger snakes."

"Carl, do you see how they've adopted them as pets? Do you see how they're exhibiting something close to love? Here's an animal that has eons of evolution telling it to run like hell whenever it sees a snake. It's so ingrained that it doesn't even matter what *type* of snake it is. There's no way a corn snake would ever attack a monkey in the wild. So this response is translated into the way the monkeys breathe, the way their hearts beat. The fear is controlled unconsciously. But not in Chicken I. Not in Chicken II, either. Don't you see, Carl? Don't you see the *point*? It's not in me, either."

"So fine. If the three of you are so alike, *you* should be playing with something that would otherwise make your skin crawl. But you don't have any pet snakes, do you Christine."

"No," I said. "I don't."

"Pickles?" I said. "Not cucumbers in general, but pickles?"

"I know it's strange," said Dr. Blau, "but some people have an irrational aversion. It must have to do with the brine. Perhaps something ancient with salt as it relates to the sea or drowning."

"So, this is Fear of Drowning, too."

"Oh, no no. Don't confuse the two. We'll do Fear of Drowning later."

He went into the locker and hauled out a five-gallon tub. Then he dropped it on the table, which caused the legs to clatter.

"But I don't have an irrational fear of pickles," I said, looking at the tub. "I like pickles. I eat pickles all the time."

"We'll see," he said. "Are you sweating right now? Let me take your pulse."

He had me open up my eyes so I could stare into his own tired ones.

"Smile," he said.

I smiled.

We'd been working with my displays of happiness, so that I might one day fear their loss.

"Arms and legs?" he said. "Normal? Any tingling sensation?"

"None," I said. "No tingling sensation at all."

"Hold out your hand."

I held my hand out. Steady-freddy.

"Okay," he says. "Go ahead. Don't look. Reach on in."

I put my hand into the tub, expecting to plunge through the flotsam of bobbing pickles and maybe feel the tickle of loose coriander and dill. Instead, it was dry all the way to the bottom. Then I felt something smooth and almost perforated, like an arm in a sequined sleeve. I grabbed hold and pulled it out—a giant, flexing snake.

"This is not a pickle," I said, holding the snake's face very close to mine, looking into its vacant eyes. Its tongue shot out and touched the tip of my nose.

"No," said Dr. Blau. "It is not. I thought I'd combine it with the element of surprise, just to see what happened."

"Have you named it yet?" I asked, as he crossed Item 7, Ophidiophobia, off the list.

Carl had me blindfolded. It was something we'd been trying, but never outside of his apartment.

"What are you doing?" I said, as I felt him leading me out the door.

"Keeping it fresh, Buttercup," he said.

He took me outside and had me stand there. It was cold. I could sense him hovering behind me, smiling at me as I wobbled, and looking at my body through my lacy underthings.

"Carl," I said.

"You're doing great," he said. "I won't let you fall."

There was a crust of snow on the railing and I grabbed through it to the metal bar beneath.

"_Bon dia_, Mees Christine," said Tiago, the Brazilian man next door, "_A neve nunca fica velha pra mim._" Across the half-wall that separates the porches, our upper-bodies were close. I was wearing only my bra on top, and I reached to pull off my blindfold, but Carl held my arms down where they were.

"Oh, no. No you don't," he said. "This way, Sweetie Pie. Surprise." He draped a sweater across my shoulders. "Here," he said. "Step into these." He bent and made a hoop of the waistband of my sweatpants, grabbing me around each calf to help me in.

"Can I see?" I said. "What's the harm in seeing?"

His knees touched the backs of my knees and pushed me forward with his strides. I'd once asked Carl to take me dancing, but he'd begged off due to rhythm. Now I felt the honesty of his refusal. He left bruises on the backs of my legs. As we moved through the parking lot, again the slush soaked through my slippers.

"I'm freezing," I said, but I'll admit that I was a little bit excited, too.

Looking back, I wish he hadn't seen me smiling.

"Right this way, right this way," he said gleefully. He skipped, first to one side of me, then the other. I could hear his keys jangle. When the car door opened, he scooped me up like on a wedding night, and dumped me in the passenger's seat.

"Oh, boy," he said, turning the engine over. I could feel the car begin to move. "Christine, Christine."

"Where are we going?" Clouds of my breath settled on the backs of my hands, making them clammy with condensation. The heating in his car had recently crapped out.

"*Scared?*" he said.

"No," I said, though if I had been, no one would have known it. Carl had convinced me, of late, to take off The Portable. I even let him disconnect the filaments at the back of my head. "I'm curious," I said, "and I'm cold. Does this surprise require that I be cold?" There was rustling in the trunk.

"No," he said. "No, it doesn't. It only necessitates you putting your party hat back on."

"Where are we going, Carl?"

I pulled the blindfold down, and this time he let me. It was getting dark, and we drove through the woods, past a semi-frozen stream that had gone milky white with ice. I had a moment of thinking that Carl was taking me somewhere to die of exposure to the elements. How strange that would be, letting my body freeze but feeling, at the same time, a heat spread through my body. A hot death, but hard as an icicle by the time a jogger found me.

"Guess," he said.

"I don't really want to guess."

I felt sad. If my metabolism slowed, if I gradually died out in these snowy woods, if my lips and fingers and nose turned blue and then white with frost, would I be afraid? All that grant money, gone to waste. The Portable useless on Carl's kitchen table. Poor Dr. Blau. He'd have to hear about it on the news.

"Shirley's!" said Carl, the name stretching through his smile. "I wrangled another invitation. Actually, it wasn't hard. Actually, she practically begged me. People pay a lot of money for the kind of entertainment I provide. Can you believe how short-sighted she was last time? I mean, I was working free, and she was pissed about an arrow hole in her wall. What did that cost her? Putty and a little bit of touch-up paint."

"Shirley's? I'm not even dressed. Look at me. And I'm in exotic underwear. Underwear that *you* asked me to put on."

"You're *fine*. That's what kind of party it is."

"An underwear party?"

"Yes!"

Carl was right. When we got to Laverne's apartment, she wrapped her bare arms around his middle. She was wearing red panties with silky red feathers attached to the hips, and a red-feathered barrette in her hair. The orange-feeders, too, were sitting on the sofa in their boxer briefs, their chests waxed for the occasion. Carl was the only one dressed, wearing his show-stopper tailcoat and bolo tie.

"You made it!" The way Laverne squeezed him, it seemed that all had been forgiven. Even the orange-feeders smiled. "And you brought Christine!" She reached to hug me, too, and I melted just a little. I have a weakness for effusive women; their attention is so rarely aimed at me.

"You got the Crenshaw?" Carl asked her.

"In the fridge," pointed Laverne. She bent and put a fold of cash in the pocket of his tailcoat.

"Gentlemen," Carl said, and the orange-feeders lifted from the sofa as if connected by a wire. They surrounded me and grabbed me by my arms and shoulders.

"What the hell?" I said, but what I really thought was, *This will be interesting.* I admit, too, that I can understand the weakness some women have for scantily clad, muscular men.

Carl took out some nylon webbing. I should have seen it coming. He'd had it in a roll in his apartment, and claimed he was making dog leashes to sell online. "Something on the side," he'd said, and I'd believed him.

"Hold her steady, boys," he told the orange-feeders. They flexed and grunted against my struggles.

Carl wrapped the webbing around my body, tying me up in knots. "Good," he spoke into my ear. "Good show, Christine. Keep it up. You're a star."

When he was through, I was wrapped tighter than a summer sausage. The orange-feeders stood around exhaling.

"Crenshaw!" bellowed Carl, and Laverne lifted a yellow melon the size of a rugby ball out of the fridge.

Carl took me by the shoulders and placed me at the wall. The arrow hole was still there from his long-ago original shot. "Cheapskate," he whispered, but to his audience he said, "The Crenshaw melon will require an act of incredible balance by my assistant. It will force me to redirect my aim at a moment's notice or else suffer the lethal consequences."

Laverne clapped and bounced up and down, causing her feathers to float. "Oh, goodie," she said. "Oh, yay."

Carl whispered, "Okay, Christine." He was being his sweet performer-self again, being patient and tender and private with me, even with everyone watching.

"Hold it together," he whispered, and I did. I stood up straight and flexed my most grounding muscles. I tried to envision the top of my head as a tabletop, and I know if I'd been shipped to finishing school, I could have balanced books up there forever.

But the Crenshaw was unwieldy. It must have weighed ten pounds. The first two times Carl placed it down, it fell right to the carpet. I thought it would burst on impact, but it held its shape.

"Unripe." Carl turned to Laverne and gave a thumbs-up. "Perfect."

"Christine," he said to me. "Let's do some visualization." He held the Crenshaw melon at his chest and gave me his best win-one-for-the-gipper stare. "This is not a Crenshaw melon . . . . This is a piece of paper." His voice went singsong. "*Just* a piece of paper." He smiled. Carl was evil then. I wanted to defeat him and his melon.

"Okay," I said. "Just a piece of paper." I closed my eyes. I visualized. "Just a piece of paper."

This time the Crenshaw stayed. I was shocked enough to smile, but smart enough not to smile too wide. I opened my eyes and saw everyone staring. I thought, *Why are they so impressed by this balanced piece of paper?* Carl was already across the room, standing next to the refrigerator. He nocked the arrow and pulled it back. The string dug against his cheek. I watched his belly rise and fall as he took aim.

One of the orange-feeders scratched his face. His eyes looked teary in the overhead light. Just like that, the piece of paper on my head turned back into a Crenshaw melon. It tipped as Carl let the arrow fly.

The Crenshaw hit the carpet and the arrow ripped a silver scar in the patch of air above my ear. Everyone gasped. Everyone but me and Carl. I was doubly sorry The Portable was on his kitchen table . . . not that I detected fear, but that fear was in the air. I thought maybe it would register, even though it wasn't mine.

"Not the fault of my aim, people," Carl said, as if to calm them down.

"Oh, the suspense is delightful," said Laverne. "Isn't the suspense delightful?" A few of the orange-feeders dropped their shocked expressions so they could nod.

"This time," Carl whispered to me, positioning my body again, "no moving. That's why we tied you up. Great theater, sure, but it also keeps you in place."

I imagined the melon again as a sheet of paper, and this time, the arrow went through clean. I stepped away from the wall and the Crenshaw hung there, bending the arrow all the way over so that its feathers pointed at the floor.

Laverne cheered.

I smiled. I waited for Carl to puff himself up and untie me so that we could do the elaborate bow we'd rehearsed together.

"And now," he said, instead, "something wild." He opened the door and winked at them. His smile would have been dashing in a high school production of *The Pi-*

rates of Penzance. "Just a second, please," he said, and went out to his car.

I stood there, bound and facing my audience. They stood there looking back at me. When Carl came in, his arms were anchored from the weight of the two plastic pet carriers he was carrying, and there came the same scratching I'd heard in the trunk on our way from the apartment. My restraints were tight—but I should have busted free. Now I have to live with the fact I didn't. A person who has no fear must always remain alert. Though bravery is not my natural state, I have no excuse for shrinking away from it. For me, at worst, it's a hot sensation, a little bit of unpleasantness. On the way over, I should have grabbed the steering wheel and swerved us off the road. I should have reached into the trunk and saved them. I should have punched Carl right in his bulbous, raspberry nose. But by then it was too late. I was tied from head to toe with nylon webbing. I was a part of his stupid show.

Carl heaved the carrying cases on the counter and stooped to bring a slice of apple to one of the metal gates.

"Here you go, you simpleton," he said, his voice in a baby-talk. "Come, come, doofus primate."

A tiny hand reached out and grabbed the apple. Then the rest of Chicken II appeared, pressed up to the edge.

"Come, come," said Carl, opening the carrier. Chicken II grabbed the cuff of his sleeve and pulled himself up the arm of the tailcoat until he was sitting on Carl's shoulders like a toddler. "This," said Carl, "is a three-year-old vervet monkey."

"*Carl.*" The name evacuated my mouth like a well-hocked ball of phlegm.

"Not to worry, Christine. Everything is under control. Chicken II and I have been *working together*."

"That's impossible," I said.

"Not impossible. Impossible to *resist*."

"Carl, put him back."

"What you failed to tell me, Christine, is how easy they are to train."

"It won't get loose in here, will it?" Laverne made a sour face and hugged her arms across her chest, backing into the living room.

"Carl, we need to get him back to the lab," I said, as sternly as I could, though I felt my voice was quavering. "He's important to the study."

"In due time." He opened the gate of the second carrier, but it appeared that it was empty. "Here Sissy, Sissy," Carl crooned. He picked up the crate and shook it upside down so that the door flapped and rattled. "I'll tell you what you *can't* train," he said. A giant snake plopped on the counter. It flexed and strained like a frenzied muscle, then curled into a pile.

There was a general intake of breath from everyone but me and Carl.

"Get. It. Out," said Laverne. She'd retreated completely to the sofa, and was being sheltered in the muscled arms of two of the orange-feeders.

"This," said Carl, picking up the snake, "is a red-tailed boa. Notice how the monkey is not freaking out. Ordinarily, it would be freaking out. But everything is under control. This is all part of the act. Right, Christine?"

What was the point of saying anything then? Laverne and her party didn't care about the unconscious fear response in monkeys. They didn't care at all about

Chicken II. They cared only, for that moment, about the ten-foot red-tailed boa Carl was draping around my neck.

"Hold him for a second, will you?"

"Oh, I can't watch," I heard Laverne say.

The snake hung from me more like a feather boa than a red-tailed one. But it was heavy enough to buckle me forward and dig the webbing of my binds into my wrists and back.

"Untie me, Carl," I said. "He's heavy."

"Wait. Wait. You're part of it."

I had a sudden craving, then—as real as a craving for something sweet—to touch the top of the snake's head. I wiggled my fingers as much as I could, and the snake raised its head to meet them. I worked over the bumps where the ears-holes must have been. It felt like the back of a hand, the tendons moving, dry.

"Ew, ew, ew," said Laverne, but my peace response was at a 10.

"There, there," I said to the snake.

Carl grabbed a barstool and put it against the wall. He lifted Chicken II off his shoulders and set him down on top of it.

He barked, "*Still*," and Chicken II stayed where he was.

Then he took the snake from off my neck and put him on top of Chicken II, wrapping the tail around those hairy shoulders to keep it all in place. The snake's head, I saw, was considerably larger than a quarter of a lime, and would be an easy shot for Carl.

"So," he said, retreating back to his position, and drawing an arrow from his quiver. "No one here likes snakes."

"Carl," I said. "*Carl.*"

The peaceful feeling rushed out of me like water from a pool. I was left with a sensation of empty, dripping cold—a sensation Dr. Blau has termed *downheartedness*, but I've never thought that was right. It has nothing to do with my heart, or with any of my other organs, either. In fact, it's a sensation that doesn't involve my body at all—just my mind that swells larger than my body ever was, and punishes me for something. "When you say 'punishes,'" Dr. Blau will ask, "punishes *how*?" and I will answer, "Just in every possible way."

Around Chicken II's shoulders, the snake started to squeeze.

"*Now, Carl,*" I said. "*Do it now.*" It was happening. Chicken II jerked his head to the left, as if something over *there* was being strangled. Poor Chicken II. He was calm. His fright response was, at worst, a 2. He didn't move again.

"*Shoot,*" I hissed. For the first time, I wanted the act to succeed. I wanted the arrow to pin that snake-head to the wall, for its tail to dangle like a flag. I wanted to take that elaborate bow we'd been rehearsing, to be unbound and walk back to the parking lot. What I didn't want was for Chicken II's eyes to bulge out, or his bowels to evacuate like a tube of toothpaste. What I didn't want was for the snake to pull tighter and tighter in. I didn't want to see Carl hesitate, or for his string-hand to shake at his cheek, his drawn arm to slowly lower to his side, the arrow unreleased.

I didn't want to see exactly what was happening, and I didn't want to think *This is all very interesting*, the way I did.

The sharp heat that filled my body was not unpleasantness; it was rage.

"*Shoot,*" I said, but it was over.

Chicken II teetered from the barstool and fell over on the floor. The snake unlocked its jaw and waggled it, positioning toward the monkey's head. I struggled in my webbing.

"Carl?" said Laverne. "Carl?"

But Carl had turned away. He was bent over the counter, attempting, to his credit, the impossible: to hide his pathetic and jagged sobs.

Self-Rated Affect Log, 7:42 PM
Feeling of Descending: 7
Disappointment Based in Gravity : 9
Heart Palpitations: ∅
Fear: ∅

"I was halfway through my notes, and you just sprinted off," says Dr. Blau. He's walking me back to the car from the Beltzerseltzer Tower, after successfully coaxing me down.

"I was dangling off the top of a 300-foot tower," I say. "I could have died, you know."

"Yes. Yes," he says. "And how did that make you feel?"

"Oh, just fine," I say.

I try not to be concerned with Dr. Blau. Instead, I think again of Carl—how he had looked just before he left me at Laverne's. I had to be cut loose from my binds by a couple of the orange-feeders. That was the last I'd spoken to him, though he still sends me pleading texts. The next day, I went to a pet store to buy another vervet monkey. It won't fool Dr. Blau for long . . . though by now, he should have noticed. The only thing he's asked is, "Are we using one monkey or two?" but maybe he's trying to frighten me. He's spoken of a *longing*-content in the fear of adults who experienced certain kinds of positive childhoods when the minds of their elderly relatives begin to go.

"Well," he says, taking me by the forearm. "I'm glad that you aren't dead."

Fear, says Dr. Blau, can come in small, almost unnoticeable episodes. A fear of compassion, for instance, in the moment it's received—a fear that it will never come again. In some ways, I understand that kind the best.

"While you were up there, I got a call," he says, "from Michelle. You remember? That nice zookeeper who helped us with the toads? They had a break-in at the exhibit."

"Oh yeah?" I say.

"Some guy just sat on the rocks for a while before they called security. A bald guy, she said."

"What'd they call *you* for?" I say.

"It's interesting," he says. "You remember what you did in there?"

"What I *did*? I sat there and looked at stuff."

"But do you remember *how* you looked?"

"*How* I looked? You mean at the toads? At the plants?"

"Yes, Christine. *How* you looked at all those things."

"I just looked. How do you look at toads?"

"Because Michelle remembers. Apparently, a bunch of the staff remembers, too. And she says this guy who broke in, the way he looked at all that stuff was just the same. Just the same as the way *you* looked. She called me to see if he was part of our experiment."

"Well, I didn't *break in*," I say. "That's a major difference."

"Interesting, is all," says Dr. Blau.

"I guess," I say, in an attempt to play it off.

Dr. Blau gets silent again, except for the grinding of his teeth. Finally, he says, "You haven't affect rated."

"I have nothing," I say, "to report."

He walks ahead of me, then swings around, his arms raised, zombie-like. "*Ah!*" he says, but not with any heart.

"Nothing," I say, looking down.

"Let's go back to the lab then," he says. "I'll run my scalpel beneath the skin of your wrists until I've flayed a three-inch square. Then I'll let you bleed until you're right on the verge of death. I won't kill you, but I'll *almost* kill you."

"Still nothing."

"Let's just go then," says Dr. Blau.

Item 17, Agyrophobia: *Fear of Crossing the Street*

We stood at mile-marker 36, at the edge of Route 70, a dozen feet behind the solar-powered emergency phone. Behind us, the maple trees had reddened. From the car, they'd looked like a wall of flame, but standing at the edge of the highway, they were all just trees again. Fall had made the air feel slick and clear. In front of us, the rushing SUVs and big rigs burned rubber and swirled up grit. Plastic bags brushed between our legs like cats.

"When you hear those jake-brakes," Dr. Blau said, "that's a good time to rate."

We'd picked this bend in the road because of the potential danger of its sharpness. To our right, in the brown grass, a cross was decorated in polyester flowers. I watched them flutter in the wind blown up by traffic. But this was not about a cross or flowers. Dr. Blau didn't want Item 17 to have anything to do with death.

"Listen to me, Christine," he said. "Death does not enter into this. This is supposed to be controlled. Let's not go mixing items. A death-experience . . . we'll get to that. I promise you. We'll get to that soon. For now, I want you on this road. Concentrate. Imagine yourself crossing, and don't think about what happens next. I don't want you thinking about the splatter. The fear should only come from the idea of crossing the street."

The jake-brakes moaned again as another eighteen-wheeler slowed for the turn. Its white metal sides fluttered as though they were made of paper.

"Now," said Dr. Blau.

I self-affect rated my fear at Ø.

Dr. Blau inched a little closer to the emergency phone, and pulled me closer with him. Though he hadn't said it, I could tell—the emergency phone was as far as he would let us go.

This was the pull-off area for the three eastbound lanes. Jersey walls divided us from the westbound traffic. On one of those walls, someone had balanced a red plastic cup—the kind Laverne might have stocked for parties.

"Look," said Dr. Blau. "Do you see it?"

"Yes," I said. "I do."

"I want you to envision yourself running across the traffic and picking that cup up off the wall." He looked at me with the sobriety of a commanding officer. "Someone needs a refill, Christine," he said. "Are you up for it?"

"Yes," I said. "I am."

"Play it over in your mind." We took a step closer. His hand was on my back, ready to catch me if I fainted, or push me if I wouldn't go. A silver tractor trailer—as slick as a seal—slowed for the curve, mourning its loss of speed with another groan. Again, I rated ∅.

"Envision your feet hitting the asphalt."

I was seeing patterns by then, seeing holes. Behind me, I imagined the trees had resumed their blazing. A highway full of smoke, blinding me, but penetrable.

And then I knew that I could make it. Nothing in front of me was made of anything hard. Those rigs, those SUVs, those buggy-looking compacts—I could pass through every one.

Across the traffic, a gust lifted the cup on its lip, but didn't make it fall.

"You see that?" asked Dr. Blau.

"Yes," I said. "It vibrated."

And as I said the word, everything seemed to vibrate around me—the leaves on the trees, the clouds above of our heads, even Dr. Blau. I saw it in his eyes.

"Self-affect rate," he said.

"Zero." *I placed my pen and clipboard in the grass.* "My fear is at a zero, still."

"Interesting," *said Dr. Blau.*

I stared at the cup across the highway and felt a ripple in the air above my head. Dr. Blau was taking notes in his corresponding log. I crouched into a runner's pose and tightened the muscles in my legs. Then, like a shot, my feet and arms began their churning. I'd crossed in front of the emergency phone before I felt the weight of Dr. Blau's body pull me down. We came crashing together at the edge of the asphalt of the pull-off lane.

"No," *he panted, and I could smell his piney after-shave. Warning horns had blared.* "Not today. God." *He let out a stream of breath and unlocked his hands from around my neck.*

"Can you imagine," *he said,* "the budget I'd need to get all these drivers to play along?"

Free Association Memory Entry:
The Time I Ran When Chicken II Died

The night Chicken II died, I ran. Just as soon as the orange-feeders cut me down and offered me a ride. I was still in my sweatpants and lacy underthings.

I ran through the concrete alleyways that link our city from neighborhood to neighborhood—those channels of slush and runoff that branch like networks of the brain. I saw the backs of rowhouses with their dim inner glows, or their pitch-blacknesses, and the backs of churches, and the backs of dry-cleaning establishments. I saw the backs of child care facilities with their mute plastic playgrounds. I ran through vacant lots and leaped over hunks of concrete the alleys had shed like piles of dirty clothes.

I ran beneath the golden globes of street lamps made misty with the coming snow. I ran beneath the piercing blue-light police cameras, and thought of Dr. Blau, watching my levels at that very moment, receiving no significant data. The Portable's wires were deaf and blind on Carl's kitchen table. What would Dr. Blau say if he knew? Recently, he'd had a change of heart about my running. "You've been running through the East Side? That's good. A woman alone at nighttime. There's bound to be a fear induction sooner or later." But sometimes he'd just say, "Be careful, Christine. Stay in the shadows. Stay out of trouble," and he'd clutch my wrist the way he'd done when I was young.

I ran with my heart pounding in my throat, but simply from my speed. I ran through the sheer human miracle of construction, miles of impermeable surface, when only a few centuries before there'd just been leaves and moss and dirt. Was the human brain mossier then, too? Before it was overlaid with all this concrete and modern thinking? I imagined the dark swampy corners of my mind which refused to be overlaid with anything?

I caught my breath atop a frozen hill, and felt a silence, thick as milk. Then I ran some more.

I ran past a building on fire. The windows were shattered, and the street was empty. I stood and watched the flames.

Would Rocko Barletta have gone inside? Would he have climbed the ashen stairs and rescued anyone within?

I ran away. Truth be told, I felt the burning all over me, felt it like a rash, like it was trying to escape from beneath the surface of my skin. An unpleasantness. It wouldn't leave me, even as I sprinted up and over, down those endless city blocks.

I ran past another fire, and another. Or maybe I ran in circles.

I stopped and breathed and concentrated. I wished I had The Portable strapped around my waist, wished that I could manipulate it in such a way to send for Dr. Blau. I'd lie to him and poison all our research, just to have him come out there and find me.

Chicken II was dead, and I was all alone. I had to catch the bus back to Carl's apartment, and wait in the snowy bushes until I saw that he was gone. I had to get Tiago to let me in so that I could grab The Portable off the barren kitchen table.

Self-Rated Affect Log 7:52 PM
 Disappointment: 9
Curiosity: 3
Stomach Twisting Realization of the Limitless Reserve
of Cruelty in Man: 7
Fear: Ø

Dr. Blau and I get back in the car, and pretty soon, I fall
asleep. This is something I rarely do. Maybe I'm wiped
out from all that climbing on the Beltzerseltzer Tower. A
dream of fiery tunnels rises behind my eyes. A father and
his girl. They're floating in a teacup, and the girl begins
to cry. A sudden patch of darkness has frightened her. I
see it. I know it. That little girl is me.

When I wake up, we're parked and sitting still.

"Sweetheart," says Dr. Blau. "We're home."

I keep my eyes closed, and pretend that I've gone on
dreaming, that Dr. Blau's voice wasn't oddly warm when
he called me "Sweetheart."

"Oh," I say. "I think I drifted off."

I look out at our lab, but our lab isn't there. Instead,
we're in some other parking lot. Some place I've seen before.

Dr. Blau unbuckles.

"Dr. Blau," I say. "Why are we *here*?"

He's already standing outside the car, and has to duck
back down to squint at me.

"You wanted somewhere else?"

"This was your office fifteen years ago." I'm about to
smile. This is where I'd come that summer, after camp
was done—my first go-round in the lab, before my time

up in the sky. When I'd come back, his office had changed. He'd moved to a nicer part of town.

He turns to stare at the front of the building. Because I'm still strapped in, I can't see the look on his face. Instead I see his fists, pushing into the small of his back, his elbows wide as if to say, "Silly me."

"Hmm," he says. "Silly me."

If I had a beard, I'd grow it as big and thick as the bushes outside of Carl's apartment—if only for times like these, to have a place to hide.

I say, "I might be feeling nervous."

"Nervous?" But he doesn't reach for his pad; he doesn't take any notes.

"Like, maybe it's getting late, and my body feels like it won't ever function the way it did at 10:30 this morning. Like I've become old and I'll never rejuvenate."

"That's just fatigue," he says, regaining his control.

"No, it's more than that," I say. "There's some *angst* or something to it."

"Fatigue can commingle with angst. Are you rating?"

"Yes," I say.

I self-affect a ∅.

Item 199, Mycophobia: *Fear of Mushrooms*

Dr. Blau had been busy cooking. The bowls were out, and the tables in the lab were all cross-hatched with vegetable peelings.

"Wait," he said, his back to me, his right elbow going mad as he worked something over with a knife. "I'm not ready for you yet."

Next to the graduated cylinders was a metal bowl of shiitakes.

I waited while he chopped.

When he turned to me, the air went out of him.

I'd popped a mushroom in my mouth.

"Oh," he said. "Never mind," and crossed Item 199 off the list.

Self-Rated Affect Log 8:02 PM
Sensitivity to the Dark: 3
Happiness: 3
Awareness of the Potential of My Own Beauty: 4
Fear: ∅

This time, the parking lot is right. I feel the correctness of the young trees with their posts and wires, the correctness of the snow banks that the plows have left behind, the dumpster with its hazmat stamps.

"Okay," says Dr. Blau. He's whispering, staring out the window. "Don't make any sudden moves."

Across the street is a new all-night daycare center, patronized by the nurses who've been working double shifts since the fires began again. There's a nurse on the sidewalk now, coming toward our car. She's pulling along her little girl, half asleep and muttering.

"I want you to watch carefully," he says. "Take notes if you have to. Pay close attention to the way their arms move. Pay attention to their faces."

There's a streetlight in the lot that sputters and casts strange shadows. Dr. Blau says, "The more frequently you see it, the better you'll understand it when it comes. Watch. Body language."

He opens the car door very quietly and crouches down next to the front tire. When the mother-nurse passes, he jumps and throws the rubber snakes he's kept coiled in his pockets.

"Snakes!" he yells.

The little girl strains back on her mother's arm, as if taken by a gale. She shrieks a sustained alarm. The streetlight flickers on and off like lightning.

"Jenny!" the nurse chokes, lifting her daughter to her arms.

At the sound of the name, Dr. Blau falls onto the pavement. I see him twitching like he's been struck somewhere peculiar in the head.

The nurse shoves her daughter behind her back and reaches to remove a shoe. It's a thick wooden platform, and she raises it up before I have the chance to move.

"No!" I yell, unbuckling. "He's a scientist!"

When I get him safe inside, he's rambling. I have to walk him with my arm around his shoulder to keep him from collapsing, and I get him prone on the examining table only by lifting with all my strength.

"Jenny," he says to me, and grabs me by the collar. I unbend each of his fingers from the fabric before I can stand up, free.

"Jenny," he says, "you're back."

"It's me, Dr. Blau. Jenny was that little girl outside. I'm Christine. Your subject, Christine."

"You're afraid," he moans. "But don't be."

"I'm *not* afraid," I say. "I'm never afraid. That's the point of all of this. I'm fearless, Dr. Blau. That's me."

"Don't be," he says. "I keep telling you."

"Dr. Blau."

"I keep telling you, Jenny. You don't need to be afraid. Even though there's every reason *to be* afraid. Every sensible reason in the world."

"You're going to be okay," I say. "You're just not feeling well right now."

"Darling," he says to me, "what can I do? What can I do for you?"

I watch him twist his face in pain. He says: "Jenny, Jenny," and flops to one side and then the other. I get my

hands on his shoulders and press him flat until his breath
starts to come back easy. "A ghost," he says, "a ghost," and
I know just what he means.

I hadn't told Dr. Blau about breaking up with Carl, but
he must have sensed the change. Maybe it was because I
was crying when I came back to the lab, but that was for
Chicken II, for having to tell Dr. Blau what had happened. He'd caught me at the door and took me to our
evaluation seats that faced the window. It was going to
snow again. He said, "It's just a ghost, fear is. You can't
hold it or see it, but everyone believes precisely in their
own revelation of its form. Look at all those nurses out
there. The world throws its greatest suffering at them,
and they take it all in stride. But they're afraid of their
mortgage payments. I hear them talk."

What I did next was strange. I started taking notes. I
picked up his pad and pen, and nodded, just the way he
nods at me. I said, "Uh-huh, uh-huh, uh-huh," making
eye contact as often as I could. I wasn't actually writing,
just making circles, but I wanted him to carry on.
"Okay," I said. "That's interesting." Here's what I sus-
pect: when it comes to actually being scared, Dr. Blau is
just as blank as me. In the same way Carl's high school
torments wiped him clean, Dr. Blau has let his queries
into other people's brains erase him into emptiness.
Though he has walked those haunted houses with me
and let those same jungle-spiders dance along his shoulders, I've never seen him squirm. Take away The Meter
and The Portable, take away Chicken I and all this self-
affect rating, and when it comes to fear, he's a man with-

out a context. Why, I wondered, did he pick *me* all those years ago at camp?

"People aren't afraid of ghosts," he said, as I scribbled out my circles. The motion was hypnotic. "Mm-hmm," I said. I listened. He said, "Fear, *itself*, is a ghost. What's a ghost, Christine? A vision? A floating head? The hint of something that has long since been buried in the ground? Does it come to us in waking or in dreams? Or was it *always* here? Does it fill up just a house? Or expand to the limits of everything we understand?" He looked at me with bloodshot eyes, and I remembered that he'd recently wanted me to self-affect rate under the influence of marijuana. He had a colleague at the University of Wisconsin who'd published on the subject. I nodded. "Listen, Christine, what are they? Huh? Ghosts? Can you tell me?"

I looked up from my notebook. "I don't know," I said. "Like Casper?"

Dr. Blau looked down and sighed.

"Casper," I said, trying to play along, "and the Ghost of Christmas Past."

"Yes, Christine," he said, and raised his head. He was suddenly reanimated. "Yes! Look at the incredible range. From poltergeists to what was basically a family pet. If that's the case, then maybe *fear* exists in all those forms, too. From anxiety to to terror to nostalgia. Maybe we've skewed the spectrum so far in one direction that we've lost our way. But you, Christine, *you're* experiencing it in different shades. Slices of the spectrum so thin they're almost invisible! So look at your potential!"

Circle, circle, circle, I scratched. "Uh-huh, uh-huh," I said.

"What is fear as we know it?" He was staring at me in that dreamy way.

"Alarm," I said. "Shock, fright, horror, panic, et cetera," I rattled off from the printouts in the log.

"Yes, but why not bliss? Why not the fear inherent in cheerfulness, enthusiasm, zeal, excitement? All the fear that's lodged in compassion? If it's all so ill-defined, why not find it in the *good*? That's what we're doing here, Christine," he said. "That's our place in this."

Now he stares with eyes so clear I have to turn my head to make sure there's no one standing right behind me.

"A ghost, Jenny," he says. "A beautiful, wonderful ghost. Oh! You came back to me."

I touch his shoulder again to keep myself from getting weak.

"I was right about that," he says. His bottom lip is wet and pink, the top one obscured by the many stray filaments of his mustache.

The phone rings and I answer it.

"Blau," says Officer P.J. Young. "It's Barletta. There's been another rescue."

"It's Christine," I say, and then, "Try to keep him there."

"I can't keep him if he wants to go. You know where all the sugar trucks park on Chase Street?"

When I turn to tell Dr. Blau, he's sleeping. Up on the aluminum table, his arm slung over his side, he looks like a body donated to science. I wait to see his chest rise and fall, and then I take his keys from out of his pocket. I try not to think of *myself* as a body donated to science. I have The Portable on. Maybe Dr. Blau will be awakened by whatever sound The Meter makes when it receives a signal. A sound he's never heard before. I hope the sound is gentle.

I'm driving when my phone vibrates on the dashboard. I hope it isn't Officer P.J. Young telling me I'm too late.

It's not. It's another text from Carl:

> Yr NOT answering yr phone ha ha Plz pick up when I call I have BIG PLANS!!! for another party @ shirleys. 4 instance thse men there will do anythng for her I dont know y So y wldnt they LINE UP TO BALNCE???? Imagine when thy all stand up well start with half limes so the bottoms r flat then 1 arrow goes thru all 6. DO NT WORRY U WLL STLL B INTGRAL!!!!

I put the phone back down and drive. Chase Street is up in smoke. The sandstone buildings flicker orange and pink across from the flames that lick the sky from the third-floor windows of the sugar building. Firemen stand tug-o-war-style at the ends of hoses and aim their spray up at the blaze. Water runs down the sides of the delivery trucks and glistens. Tomorrow their flat roofs will be weighted down in ice.

I step out of the car and gasp. The air is sharp inside my throat and smells of burning syrup. The low-hanging clouds are black.

Officer P.J. Young has his hand raised and comes tiptoeing in my direction. "Christine," he says, and I walk to him, though I don't get very far. The pavement is thick with goop. At each step, my heels pull from my shoes.

"He's here," he says.

"Barletta?" I ask, but P.J. Young doesn't seem to be taking things seriously. He makes a sound that's like a giggle.

"Watch," he says, taking his fingers and running them over the bricks in the wall of the sugar building. He sticks his fingers in his mouth. "Try," he says.

The bricks are sticky and warm from the fire inside.

"Taste," he says, and I do: molasses.

"They keep delivery bags on all three floors. It burned and they watered it. All we need is carbonation." This close, I can see it oozing from the windows, running down the walls in viscous channels.

"Where is he?" I say, thinking of Dr. Blau laid up on that table—of bringing him home this piece of good news like a healing tonic.

My phone buzzes again.

> Yr prob wondring re your role in show. LETS TALK!!! U stll hve a lot 2 offer re fear. Can we get tall platfrm in apt?? Or muv show outsde?? I wll luk in2 ampthtr avlblty

P.J. Young waggles a finger at the distance. "There," he says. "You see him?"

"That one?" I ask, and he says, "Yeah."

Barletta is leaning his back against a squad car, pressing his palms into the hood. Even in this cold, his bald head is pouring steam, cooling from the rescue.

"What'd he get?" I ask.

"Not much he *could* get, a few bags of sugar is all."

"Well," I say. "That won't be hard to beat."

"What?" says Officer P.J. Young.

I must have twitched or something, because he says, "Easy now, Christine." But I'm still just staring, something holding me down in place. I expected Barletta to be broader—an ex-boxer with lean, rangy muscles.

I squint to see more clearly. In recent months, Dr. Blau has sent a call out to photographers. He doesn't want the wails or shrieks of photojournalism, but the moments that precede a body's reaction to the horror that it's seen—just *the moment of induction*, as the skin tightens at the base of the skull. Dr. Blau has shown me hundreds of these pictures, from all around the world, but it's not until I see Barletta staring into the fire that I realize what they share—a precursor to the wailing and shrieking and covering up of eyes—and it's what Rocko Barletta is doing now. He's *concentrating*—and seems as likely to dissolve into a pure quivering mist of focus as to seek out another fire. But this is very strange . . . He's concentrating *after* the event.

"Not what you'd expect from a hero, eh?" says Officer P.J. Young.

"Well . . . ." I say.

If Barletta's not heroic, he certainly is *familiar*—bald as a marble and *bird-boned*, I think. Flap-jointed. Short sleeves even on a night like this, exposing red, knobby elbows. A man who hardly looks capable of drawing a bowstring to his ear.

"*Copycat*," I say, lurching in his direction.

"Wait, wait," says Officer P.J. Young with a hand on my arm to hold me back.

The shadows of Barletta's jaw begin to dance, and my voice jams in my throat.

Something in Officer P.J. Young accedes, and he nods in Barletta's direction. "Be good," he says. "Okay? Just take it slow. Don't scare him off."

But I can't. Barletta turns his head and I see his face in profile. He's still sweating from the flames, the hollows of his cheeks glistening in the streetlight. His nose tapers to a point—arrow-like—and I imagine his face flying at me to take that sofa cushion off my head.

I try to grab my phone, but my fingers have all gone numb, though the world around me is speeding up. A kid in a puffy jacket walks up to the wall and cups his hands beneath the syrup. He looks over his shoulder and nods back to his friends. In no time there are three, four, a dozen children in winter hats, creeping through the shadows, stepping over fire hoses, and pressing their hands up to the wall. I see them tasting from their naked, dripping fingers.

Officer P.J. Young sees them, too.

"Hey," he says *"Hey."* He strides toward them, a grownup with the law and personal hygiene on his side.

"Mr. Barletta," I shout, and what he does next is proof he's just like me.

He runs.

I watch him bolt down the street into an alley. Dr. Blau's car is at the curb, but I don't have any time for that. Anyway, a car is not the thing for chasing through an alley.

"Hey," I yell, echoing P.J. Young.

I can see his long legs pumping, his marble head holding almost perfectly still. He has the stride of a distance runner, and I chase him through the concrete channels between brick buildings, these alleys that are ashed in snow. I see his pants, his arms, the sides of his shoes as he slips around each bend. My feet are soaked in city-slush, cold grit in my socks that will forevermore be gray.

"Stop," I call, forgetting myself. *"Police."*

He leaps a fence.

When I try, the toe of my shoe catches in the chain, and I land funny on my knee. He goes down a street filled with puddles of black water, and when I splash, the water goes up my calves. I start to shiver. I run harder just to warm myself up.

At the next turn, I catch a glimpse of the billow of his shirt, the white rubber sole beneath a shoe. Another ten strides and he's gone.

"Barletta," I huff, my hands on my knees. "Rocko," I say. "Come. Back."

I'm wet and shivering, out alone on the street. Everything is closed but Chinese restaurants with bulletproof ordering areas. I find one and go inside. It's warm in there, and the floor is muddy with footprints. I pick the chair leaking the least amount of stuffing and huddle myself in a corner. My teeth will not stop chattering. I think to self-affect rate a Ø, but my phone starts buzzing again.

> I purchasd red sequind dress 4 u. asked if it wld be gd dress 4 assistnt. Lady sd its an asistnts dress lol like she knows. U cn gess d pain this purchse has put on my lif!! THIS IS GENROUS ACT!!! I NEED $ 2 EAT!!! 4real luk what I did for you. Its big. I smell the shirt u left behind 24/7. It smells like u.

"Order?"

There's a voice behind the bulletproof glass. A woman in an apron has her eyebrows raised.

"Just warming up," I say, rubbing my hands together and vibrating my shoulders to indicate the intensity of my shivers.

"Leave," she says, and points to the door with the fat end of a baseball bat.

Outside, another message:

Tiago sez I'm n luv wit you lol. Lke he knows!! He says quando ficara quente n thts the hart of r problm. such a beautful language he cud tlk re weather & sound like luv sonnts. How bout these cats they have @ mall??? Theyr stuffed so thy luk real n they have battery so they breathe like real cats, or do peopl get mad wen shooting even fake cats????

I turn my phone off and think to drop it in a puddle, but I do something else instead. I walk. It's night but I move slowly. I realize that I'm lost, and running will just lose me deeper. I'll find a bus and take it some place warm.

Down an alley, two kids are crouched and throwing dice against a wall. They're no older than eleven. It's a cold, dark night on a deserted street. They are exhibiting a kind of bravery. They have, at least, potential.

"What are you two doing?" I ask in my best school-teacher's voice. "Shooting craps?"

"Oh, we're just practicing," one of them says, without looking up at me.

As I get closer, I see that what they're throwing are small pieces of white stone, the kind filched from some-one's driveway.

"You're not practicing with *those*, are you?" I say.

"We don't have *real* dice," he says, and I'm touched. I think of all those charities across the ocean, when right here in the USA, kids don't have real dice to practice with.

I should scoop them up and take them home—the kids, I mean—and turn the lab into something useful—a recreation center or casino. Two more of their friends are coming down the alley.

But they're older. Teenagers, or maybe in their twenties.

"Who's this pregnant lady?" one of them asks.

I look down and see The Portable bulging through my shirt. "I'm not pregnant," I say.

"Hmm," he says, considering. "Odd having a pregnant lady out here at night."

They're tall, both of them, much taller, I realize, than me.

"Bradley," he says to one of the young craps practitioners. "Time to go home." To me, he says, "They have a report due tomorrow. The eruption of Mount Pinatubo, and do you think they've even started? They lack time management skills. Wasting half the night talking to a pregnant lady."

I lift my shirt to show them what's beneath, proof that I'm in no way expecting. The Portable's LED display flickers in the dark.

Chastened, the craps practitioners flicker, too, and run off into the shadows.

The older boys step in closer to me, staring at The Portable as though it were a belt buckle of confounding proportions.

"What in the world?" says the one concerned with time management.

"It's a device for monitoring fear," I say. "I'm part of an ongoing experiment."

"A scientist!" he crows.

He's near enough to touch me.

He touches me. Right on my stomach, on the skin above the wires. His fingers are warm.

The silent one steps behind me and I'm hedged in by their bodies. If I were to self-affect rate right now, I would not be happy. I would not be anxious or curious, either. Everything down the line would be at Ø. For the first time in a long time, I am not interested in what comes next.

"Take it off," the formerly silent one says.

"I can't," I say. "It's sending data to a lab right now. I'd interrupt the transmission."

Suddenly, I'm wrapped up in his arms. Some kind of wrestling move I can't escape. I struggle, but he's strong. The one in front yanks the cords from off my waist. Suction cups come unstuck, and a searing pain rushes from my skull down through my spine. They've disconnected the filaments they couldn't possibly have known existed. I double over and up comes lunch, all over the clean, white sneakers of the thief in front of me. "Ungh," he grunts, observing his spattered shoes. "I can't escape eruptions!" He slaps my shoulder, open-handed, more a warning against more puking than a blow.

I throw an elbow hard into the one holding me from behind. He's padded by his jacket, but I've hurt him, just the same. The one in front stumbles forward, and I raise my knee and catch him in the stomach. The Portable is facedown on the street. He picks it up and runs. "Eruptions!" he calls out behind him. I see him go and then I don't. My vision isn't good. I'm being wrenched back and forth by the one who still has me in his grip.

He squeezes and shakes and I feel my feet lift off the ground. He shakes me until the tip of his nose grazes one of the holes in the back of my head, and hot sparks of pain crackle behind my eyes. I slide a foot behind his legs, throw my hips toward him, and he tumbles. We land in an icy puddle. I'm soaked to the bone and freezing again. And maybe, I think, *this* will be the time I die of it, but if I'm going down, at least I'll go down swinging. I ball my fists, but he stands and spits out something that might just be a tooth. Then he disappears back down the alley, where if things go well he'll be a boon to Bradley and his schoolwork.

I get up. The Portable is lost, but I am still alive and unafraid.

Two people have been watching the final moments of this episode. An old woman and a younger woman, standing on a marble stair. They are smudges in the darkness.

"You alright, ma'am?" the older woman says. "I called the police, but don't hold your breath that they'll show."

"I'm cold," I say, and mean it. I'm vibrating like a beaten drum, and the woman walks up the stairs into her house before reemerging with a coat. I put it on. The sleeves come halfway up my arms.

"What will *he* wear?" I ask, thinking of the child it belongs to.

"Clarence? That boy runs hot. Anyway, he's more of an inside cat these days. Been in his room all evening, working on some volcano project."

"Thank you," I say, and turn to run. I'll make it up to Clarence later. Better to be lost quickly and find my way again, than to be lost for the rest of the night.

Ahead, I find a bus stop. Men stand around in stocking caps and stiff cotton jackets ready for a late shift. A woman my age with her hair done up, fur at her collar, pops her gum like gunshots.

In the bus, I'm finally warm, and I think of what it's like being Clarence, who doesn't wear a coat. In the seat beside me is an old man with whiskers.

"Hello," I say. "My name is Christine Harmon. Do you mind if I ask you a question?"

"Not at all," he says. His face is patched with scabs, and he looks at me uneasily. I wonder where I am.

"How would you feel if you'd just been assaulted in an alleyway? If you had to rate your fear on a scale from zero to ten?"

He lifts his bottom lip to touch the tip of his nose, deciding whether or not I'm teasing. A grown woman in a child's jacket, dirty and wet and with questions.

"That'd be pretty scary," he says. "Ten's the highest? Ten, I guess."

"Even," I smile, "a brave guy like you?"

"Maybe eight, then. What's a nice young lady like you doing on a *bus* this time of night?" he asks. "Doesn't your boyfriend have a car?"

I close my eyes and fall asleep, and when I wake the streets are all familiar. I'm back in a part of town where nothing is on fire.

Once, there was running away to join the circus—all the way to Paramus, NJ. There was coming home to parents who loved me, to our cat Blackie, who was an indoor cat until she went outside to die. There were pork chop and applesauce dinners after all my homework was done.

And then there was none of that anymore.

I was fourteen, and it was the winter after camp. I was in school, and I had just walked on a third-story ledge to retrieve a paper football.

Our principal, Mr. Becker, told my parents I'd become a danger to myself—a phrase he must have heard somewhere on the news. The school didn't have a psychologist then. Mr. Becker was our psychologist. "She has those burns on her hand," he'd said. "They're still pretty bad. And now those bandages on her head. The other students make comments. It's hard for a girl her age."

No one had ever made a comment, but my parents were concerned. They took me to a dermatologist who held my hand and flopped it over like she was observing the curious markings on a fish. "Really," she said, "there's not much to be done. Does it hurt you still?"

"Yes," I said. Where the stove had burned me, parts of my palm were hard and smooth as wax. But each day I felt the heat there less and less. It had gone from raging in my body to settling in the flesh at the bottom of my thumb.

"Let me take a look at that noggin," the dermatologist said, but I'd pulled away, not letting her touch the stitches in my forehead.

"Nothing to be afraid of," she said, and my father did something interesting. He pulled me close. I could feel the warmth of his sweater, how his chest had heated it up. I can still feel it now. "She's all better," he told her. "She can be afraid."

"Pardon?" the doctor said.

"The stitches are coming out soon," he said. "We're really here about the hand."

The dermatologist looked confused. Then she took my hand again. "The scarring will diminish," she said. She'd bent down, hands on knees to speak to me, and made her face hopeful when she looked up at my parents. "By the time you go to college, you'll hardly even see it."

But she was wrong. By the end of the year, my hand looked just the same. And like a taunt, I could barely feel the heat. It was my memory of the fireplace—its wonderful spreading warmth—that faded, as would the memory of Paramus, NJ, and Blackie the cat, who'd died beneath those tires.

I'd needed someone to talk to. I needed someone to *tell*.

I was still a kid, but I'd make conversation with old men on the bus. They were the best for telling because they were so ready to hear the things I said. Those old men—those wonderful old men!—were like dried-out sponges, just waiting for something to pour out of me. They'd let me talk for their fifteen-minute ride from Parkville to Lake Walker, or Waverly to Sandtown, or Medfield to Govans, like I was water running from a long dead pipe. There was gratitude in their listening—me, Christine, a wonder. I'd say to them, "My name is Christine Harmon," like I was nine years old and not fourteen. What did they know from children's ages? "Would you mind if I ask you a question?" They'd smile, readying themselves for one of those fuzzy-edged grandfather-moments they'd been preparing for their entire lives, and I'd say, "How would it feel if you looked at something really closely—" I'd look around, pretending to search for something, though I knew what I would choose: the fabric on the seat in front of me, because I'd been staring at it already, and because I'd found that if I focused on something, anything, hard enough, I could make all my memories disappear. I'd say, "Like the fabric on this seat here. This *strip* of fabric, specifically. Suppose you concentrated on it—I mean *really* focused your eyes—and then all of a sudden you couldn't remember anything you'd ever done in your entire life."

The old-timer would be confused, and would search out a new strategy for dealing with me.

"Well," he'd say, with gravel in his voice, "I suppose that'd be pretty strange," and he'd collect himself, trying to escape me now, though he'd already given me my answer.

I came to understand that when I thought I was experiencing fear, I was really experiencing something else. I'd wait for the blood to pump into my ears, or for my pulse to race, but when it did, it was only because I was sprinting. My skin did not crawl, and when the goosebumps came, it was from a moment on a movie screen. I was often curious. I touched a rat that was trapped at the bottom of our garbage can and let it bite my finger. The tang of unpleasantness made me think that I was getting close to something new. I waited for fear to come. I looked at the rat. My finger hurt, but that was all. I wasn't afraid of pain.

And so I jumped from our roof to the boxwood hedge beneath, covering myself in tiny cuts. I held myself underwater at the community pool. The lifeguards were not amused. A looseness overtook my days, and the joints of purpose that connected me to my future threatened to come unhinged. My grades dropped, too. I became quiet. My happiness dulled until I was experiencing only the passage of time.

I cut school more often—it was easy; I was practically grown—and stayed home to watch TV. Game shows, mostly. At commercial breaks, I'd brush my teeth, again and again. I'd wipe down the counters for my mother, and put cans of soup on the stove. After three hours, the boredom was like a numbing agent. Not even lunchtime yet. How many days had I done this? Six? Maybe twelve; I lost count. If I'd created a self-affect rubric for myself back then, my Helplessness levels would have been elevated. Had I only known. The acceptance of helplessness, Dr. Blau says now, is a salve for many fears. *Relinquishing* is something I'm supposed to avoid. But to be powerless is often pleasant.

But back then, watching game shows, the house was always cold.

One day, I walked down to the business park, just to get some air. A group of ladies stood in the parking lot, smoking cigarettes.

"Got a light?" I said, and one of the ladies reached over with a flame.

I didn't smoke, but in my pocket was a receipt I'd kept from the Pic n' Save. I lit it on fire and thanked the ladies.

They didn't seem to notice. Giving someone a light was as meaningless as nodding hello.

I walked away with my hand cupped around the burning piece of paper. It was burning very quickly, and when it had blackened and curled almost to my fingers, I traded the receipt for a dried leaf, holding one against the other. The leaf burned just as fast. I had to stop moving forward, right there, and pass it from one dead leaf to another. Then I found a Chinese menu stuck behind a mailbox flag. That burned slower, and I got another half block watching the green letters of Moo Goo Gai Pan turn to ash from orange flame, crumbling and fluttering away. I bent to strip an unread morning newspaper from its plastic sheath. That lit up like a torch, and I jogged and carried it out in front of me. I was excited. Some small part of my brain was transported back to sitting in front of our wood-burning stove, and I floated, amniotic, in the pleasure.

When the paper sputtered and drooped, wads of flame fell to my feet. I found a clothesline and burnt a house dress at the end of a stick. The synthetic fabric made the flames turn pink and green. The sleeves and flowered folds had seemed to vibrate.

How can I express how it felt to walk home with that burning stick held just out from my body? Only minutes before I'd envisioned the rest of my day in the hour-long segments of daytime shows. By extension, it hadn't been difficult to see my whole life meted out that way—mornings of *The Price is Right* to evenings on the *Wheel*. But that house dress had me buzzed. I was like those parking lot ladies, chain smoking, lighting the end of one thing off the next. So it was natural that when I walked into my parents' garage, I dipped the flame end of the stick into a bucket full of rags. It was natural that I stepped back and watched the fire jump and dance without thinking I'd created an emergency.

I'd stood and warmed my hands. As the heat came on, I'd let the cold escape from every pore.

My father never parked his car in the garage. Instead, he used it as a shop. He'd built a large wooden workbench. In a moment, it was a bench of flame. A box of my mother's winter clothes went up, and then her stack of wrapping paper. The plastic around each tube bubbled up like soap. It became evident to me that there was suction in the room, pulling everything toward the heat. It seemed that pulling back was necessary, but I just stood and waited. What would happen if I just let go? Only death. If I, myself, ran into those flames, all I would do was die. But the flames did not pull me in. They pulled in everything else. A can of solvent exploded, sending chunks of fire-liquid in the air. A vacuum cleaner—the bag of dust sizzling but never catching fire. My father's hat collection in the rafters. The rafters. The extra table we kept up there, slowly, like an overnight log, deepened and pulsed with red.

My father had already arrived from work. He'd come through the house, and opened the door to find me.

"Christine?" he said. "Oh God, Christine!"

I felt I needed to shed light on what was happening, but I should not have lifted the mechanical door. I should have known that that was not the way to cool a fire.

Alas, for all my hindsight.

I pressed the button and the door groaned up, one panel at a time.

There was a great whoosh of wind and flame and I heard my father shrieking, and I was hairless from the time the police questioned me right up through the hearing. Hairless, but—they told me—lucky to be alive.

Self-Rated Affect Log, 9:47 PM
Faith in the Kindness of Strangers: 5
Disappointment in the Kindness of Strangers: 5
Curiosity: 8
Fear: ∅

Dr. Blau is back on his feet, wearing a clean white lab coat. He's playing with some droppers.

When he looks at me, he fumbles and squeezes blue solution on his knuckles.

"Your lip is fat," he says.

"I got knocked in the face."

"You're all muddy."

"I fell."

"You're shivering."

"I walked here from the bus stop."

"What about my car?"

"Do you remember me taking your car?"

He frowns at my midsection. "What happened to The Portable? Don't tell me you left it in the car. P.J. Young called. And how did you detach it? Christine," his eyes are piercing. "I've told you this before. Outside a sterile environment, the risk of infection . . ."

"I got mugged. It was stolen. It's gone forever."

"*What?*" he says, and I can tell—though he'd deny it— that the person he's angry with is *me*.

"It's gone," I say. "I was almost killed again."

"Killed?" He perks up and clicks his pen. "Sit down, Christine. While it's fresh. Good lord. Let's go over the checklist. Big ones first: Terror? Panic? Give me an affect rating."

I turn to leave, though I'm not sure where I'll go.

"Christine?" He looks at me from his chair, eyebrows raised, expectant and smiling, like he's sure that whatever comes next will be good.

"I think I'm through," I say. "I think I might be done with this."

"Done?"

Chicken I is rattling his cage like he does when he thinks that we have food.

"What do you mean 'done'? This last experience could be illustrative."

"I was in danger."

He thinks. "I've been trying hard to protect you, but maybe that's been a mistake."

Dr. Blau has done so much—carved out a place for me here in the lab. For so long, I'd wandered without a home.

"I don't know," I say to him, "what to say about that."

"No," he says, and his fingers begin to shake. His face is not quite right. "Don't leave me here like this."

After the hearing, my mother stayed away. I guess she'd had enough. It was interesting. I thought she'd known very little—the paper football incident, sure, and my burning down her house. But she must have known much more. Whatever strangeness that had hovered around me must have spread through our home like the smell of gas. Then the fire blew everything up—a ball of flame that destroyed all evidence of her parentage. Why would she reclaim it? Why would she want to reconstruct anything that she'd made? She had a chance to set out on her own again.

Since there was no house to live in, and no one grown to call the shots, I went to work. What else could I do? I answered an ad in the paper thinking, _No way. No way they'll give me this_—but then they did. Actually, they referred me to a contract crew who referred me to a parking lot. There I found Raoul. Raoul was smoking a cigarette and picking paint from off his fingers. In the back of his pickup, his tools were scattered on a cloth.

"You old enough to work?" he said, and I said, "Yeah."

"And heights are not an issue?"

"Not for me."

For the first time in a long time, I was eager.

"Well, I got to interview you," he said, and he scratched the base of his neck where the word _Bulldog_ was tattooed in cursive letters. His fingertips, lips, the corners of his eyes, his hairline—everything was stained or cracked or peeling—everything crusted up in gunk.

He was young though, much younger than my parents. Not really much older than me.

"See these tools? I want you to pack 'em all up in those boxes and then put 'em back up in my truck." He pointed to several metal tackle boxes. "Then we'll see what's next."

Though it was very cold, he wore a thin thermal top, and when the wind blew his hair around, I saw that the tips of his ears were blue. He cupped his hand to re-light his cigarette and nodded. "Get to it, then," he said, and walked into the warming trailer.

I hustled to pick up all his hammers and tape measures and boxes of screws, to arrange their asymmetries in the tackle boxes so the lids would clamp down shut. It was not very difficult. When the firefighters waded through the wreckage of our house, they found holiday lights melted together that looked like a Rubik's cube. The packing had been my handiwork. For years, I'd been assigned the chore of arranging my mother's boxes, sorting through our jumbled seasonals so that they stacked together neatly. Compared to our family's Valentine's decorations, putting away those tools was a breeze.

"Hi ho, Silver," Raoul said, rubbing his bare hands on his pants. "That was fast. I'm Raoul and you're hired."

We worked together on the bridge, painting the Westbound span. Raoul was impressed by what I had to offer. On our cigarette breaks, he'd launch into permutations of the same old question, grinning as he asked them. "You scared?" he'd ask, as the wind blew us all around, and later, "How about *now*?" We stood in our half-cage, rigged up in harnesses, dangling ten feet below the rumbling traffic, 130 feet above the whitecaps on the Bay. It didn't take Raoul long to unclip one of the carabiners on my harness so that my connection to the bridge was more precarious. I'd hang my arm through the cage and let the wind fill up my mouth. It wasn't long after that that he unclipped both, testing what I'd do. Soon I was free-climbing, freaking him out.

"Okay, okay, okay," he'd say, as though plunging to my death might get him into trouble. But I heard something quiver in his voice. It was more than nerves. The quiver didn't come from anything he thought he knew, nothing concerning the wind or rope or velocity of my body as it might hit the surface of the water. It came from some-where submerged within him. I imagined dropping a line from where we stood, 130 feet up, and sinking it an-other 100 feet into the Bay. I imagined an ancient, gnarly pike taking my worm, swimming with the bait in its mouth in slow and certain circles. What would I have felt of that, all that way up where I was? Just a quiver, a strange and distant tug. Raoul's quiver was a bit like that.

"Okay now, Miss Christine," he'd say. "Let's buckle you back up."

Raoul was a Mohawk Indian, or at least he claimed to be. He looked like a kid I'd known in school named Jimmy Lyle, though as far as I knew, the Lyles were not Mohawk Indians.

But I learned where not to press him. Instead, I went right on handing him his paint scrapers and brushes when he needed them. I was his assistant. He needed both his hands to get the tough spots, and to maneuver on the platform in the cage. Sometimes he needed both his hands just to grab the safety bar and keep from blowing away.

Once, I let myself be blown away. After I'd heard that quiver in his voice, I wanted to hear it again, and on a gust from the south, I spread my arms and let it catch the fabric of my jacket. I let it lift my feet off the wire floor and pin me to the cage.

"Okay, okay," he'd said, but dropped to his knees and grabbed my feet, to anchor me back to the bottom. "That's enough, Christine."

He stopped unclipping my carabiners after that, and looked at me, always, from the corners of his eyes. Sometimes, his hands would shake while he painted, and I felt bad for teasing him. He was no real bulldog, my Raoul.

Soon I was sleeping in his trailer. Where else did I have to go? Raoul was good to me. We cooked on a stove that was just an empty tuna can filled with sterno, lit up with a match. It took an hour for our rice to boil, but Raoul made sure I ate. At night, he laid his weight into me as if getting back at gravity for tugging on him all day. I felt he might crush my organs, crush my bones. It was a miracle I could stoop so easily to the supply bucket the next morning, that I could always hand him a newer, softer brush. When he pressed into me like that at night, I read his tattoos to keep from crying out. Many were animal names. Along with *Bulldog*, he had *Gator* and *Wolf* and *Tasmanian Devil*. He had the faces of five women, like mug shots, lined across his shoulder blade. We were quiet when we talked because Tony and Chick, who were painting the Eastbound span, also lived inside that trailer. They hadn't known each other, and they hadn't known Raoul. It was the bridge that made them bunkmates. Chick and Tony said they were Mohawk Indians, too. "You're one of us now, kid," Chick said to me. "Just don't pull a Geronimo on us, alright?" He looked warily at Raoul. "That's the deal, okay?"

The bridge was beautiful, and the Bay beneath it, a mirror full of spite. It rumbled up its colors from the deep, and broke up the reflections of the sun when it was so inclined. When the clouds were gray, the chop was gunmetal, though sometimes there was no chop, sometimes it was flat as glass that melted around the tankers, their wakes expanding into quicksilver. I did not trust the Bay. *Isn't it interesting*, I thought, how it swallows up, how it can open and reseal, how it pretends to have no *memory* of what has cut it open. Isn't it interesting how it could take Raoul from me.

Soon, we'd finished the Westbound span, and Raoul became excited. He'd envisioned a life for us together. "Chrissy," he said. "This is good, this is *good*. Tomorrow we'll take the bus to Paramus. I've worked up there before. They have nice trailers. Everything under the table."

But I did not want to go back to Paramus. Tony and Chick were already there, laying tar on the New Ridgewood Bridge. I could get a job anywhere, I thought, but it would be without Raoul. I'd been thinking, *Raoul is nice, but Chick and Tony are nice, too.* Part of me was thinking that there were nice people everywhere, that every dot on the map was just another concentration of where they'd gathered. But not Paramus. All Paramus held for me was runaway dreams without a circus.

In the morning, we walked to the Greyhound station. I even bought a ticket. My guilt response was at 9.5 or 10. After all, Raoul had taken me in. Maybe he'd even loved me a little bit. We got onboard and sat down in those high-backed seats upholstered in neon squiggles. Just before the doors closed, I got up and stood in the aisle. I raised my arms to stretch. Raoul was so excited he was already staring out the window. I arched my back and stretched a little more. I made a stretching sound.

"I guess I'm done with all of this stuff," I said, thinking it best to tell him that it was the *business* I was over.

"Huh?" he said. Outside were other buses and a huddle of rusted dumpsters. Across the street, a business for rental cars.

I continued standing as the driver made the announcement to take our seats, and as he released the brake and started to roll. I continued standing as we pulled out of the lot . . . and then I was running down the aisle.

Is there anyone left on planet Earth who doesn't know how to release that door? I did it so quickly—pulling the lever—that the driver didn't flinch. Did he even notice? Did he even care? I was out on the street and barely jostled, while the bus was signaling to make a left, and then while it pulled into the stream of northbound traffic. Then I was on the street and walking, and Raoul was still inside.

I looked up at the windows. The streaks of reflection shot my guilt response as high as it had ever been. But there was no going back. There would be no Paramus for me.

I'd saved enough cash for other bus tickets—enough to survive in other towns. I had a gift for the work, the way I could flourish so high up in the air. Bridge people could see it right away.

So I bought another ticket to another city, and I worked that job until I left it. I bought another ticket, and another, and so on.

I was hired. Again and again, I was hired.

I'd take a job on a bridge in Wadmalaw, or one in Whetstone. I'd find scaffold work in Philly or D.C. They'd take me up a building that looked out on the city. I'd work until I got tired of the job, or things got slow. All across this great country, there are people overhead. I'd begun my wanderings in the sky. There were windmills to maintain in Kansas, turbines in Montana to be cleaned. Roofs always needed patching, but what was a roof to me after that thousand-foot transmission tower I'd climbed in Pocatello? Anyway, the roofers I met were animals. A ladder's length off the ground and in no time they'd come unmoored. When the wind pulls at your joints, the rules of the world below can come to seem like petty squabbling. It was easy to be brash.

I went up taller things. There were skylines to explore. Whole landscapes to regard from up above. I looked down onto lakes that curled into toxic brown inlets—highways and cloverleafs, woods that creased around thin country roads. As we climbed, the tangled floss of telephone wire became thinner and thinner, and then finally disappeared. I looked out at fingernails of bright white sand. The crust of one wave and then another. Water that went from clear to blue to so dark it blackened. There were spotty green parks that clung like mange to the bellies of cement cities. Clouds like bullet-trails. Checkerboard fields and traffic, traffic, traffic. Swimming pools were bits of sapphire jewelry. Layers of brick, and slanted rooftops, and unslanted rooftops. Layers of parking lots, and layers of leaves on trees on distant hilltops. Yellow buses and green buses and blue buses. Double-decker buses that did not look double-decker at all, not from where I was perched. Glass buildings that turned to gold at sunset. Neon lights and cranes. Unsym-

pathetic thoughts, which would not leave me.
Nightscapes like brain scans—lights flashing, and lights
sustained. Wonder. As the sun came up, I'd see the early
people. The air would be grainy enough that particles in
the atmosphere seemed to float like clouds of gnats. The
light was right for that. I'd see one person breathing out,
passing that breath to someone else, breathing in. Sometimes, there were fireworks in the distance, always in the
distance. Balloons with baskets and people inside. Ban-
ners holding steady behind one-man planes. Ads for
weight loss solutions in the sky. Smog and spires. Clouds
moving in, and rain like swaths of static. Lightning.
Wind coming to yank at my shoulders. To remind me.
Then calm. Everything empty and quiet. I can't remember everything, or else I've never tried to separate it out.
Who remembers one cloud from the next? I traveled, I
worked. The years went by. And that was enough for me.
It had all been very interesting. But the place I was was
never my home.

It was because of that that I came back here, looking
for Dr. Blau.

I'm halfway out the door when Dr. Blau wraps me up in something between a tackle and a hug. I've seen him use this technique before when Chicken II got loose. One hand is behind my neck, and the other pulls me tight at the waist where The Portable should be. I make it easy for him, and he frog-marches me to the parking lot to stand in front of his empty space.

"Damn," he says. "My car."

Even clutched as I am in his arms, I can feel that his strength is tinged with something strange. I think of Raoul—how he got the jitters when he thought I'd be blown away. Dr. Blau and I might just as well be up a dozen stories off the ground.

We take the bus.

He pins my wrists behind my back—though gently, gently—as he guides me up the steps. The bus driver looks at the ticket machine instead of looking at us. Dr. Blau uses the hand not engaged in pushing me forward to pay our one-way passes. *Pushing* is not the word, but if anyone were looking, that's the word they'd use. I make it easy for him, still.

I think: *Maybe this is not actually happening the way I think it's happening. Maybe it's another item on the list—abduction on a bus.* <u>Item 446</u>: *Fear of Realizing You Don't Really Know Someone You Thought You Knew Quite Well. Maybe he's monitoring my fear response right now. Wouldn't that be interesting.* I don't make a fuss because of what might be his scientific plans. I've been shown countless pictures of stoic faces, so I know how to cinch my mouth and steel my eyes.

We sit near the back.

"Where are we going?" I ask, but Dr. Blau just stares out the window into the darkness. Soon, beyond the walls of the highway, the air is lit with the parking lots of giant stores. We have left the city. I look at Dr. Blau with my eyebrows raised, a look of bemusement that no kidnapping victim has ever employed. I am not afraid. Or at least, I feel no real change.

Not that Dr. Blau has noticed. He's looking at the back of his hand—squinting as if to expunge a blemish with the severity of his concentration. The way his lips crack and quaver remind me of my bus rides long ago.

"Hi," I say to him now. "My name is Christine Harmon. Can I ask you a question?"

He pries loose his gaze and stares at me without speaking.

"How would you feel if you'd just been taken from a laboratory against your will and placed on a bus to an undisclosed location?"

He blinks and opens his mouth a little.

"Afraid?" I ask. "On a scale from zero to ten."

"Jenny," he says. "Please. I don't want you to be afraid."

Okay. Fine. He's calling me Jenny again. It makes my stomach clench the way the Big Devil—with all its loops and drops—never could. If this is all just detail for the realism of our experiment, it's detail I don't yet understand. I am not more fearful when he calls me Jenny, only more confused.

My phone vibrates:

Were r U? I lukt @ lab u are not @ lab!!! Com over ill show you the bizness. You knw how I get whn I dnt c u, u get that way 2. If I have 2 tlk to Tiago agn re love ill shoot myslf with my arrow. Fnny thing, tho. Tiago volnteerd 2 b in show. Wants to b tide up w u I sd ok!!! I know u dnt really care. Nthing 2 b afrd of. Jst Tiago.

The bus turns into a neighborhood. It has snowed here more recently or else the heat of the city fires hasn't traveled this far north. Tree branches are as fat as arms in white wool sweaters, and the bushes in front of houses are capped in ice.

My phone says:

Where r u chris

My phones says:

Hve the red dress. U will lk bettr than yuv evr lkd!!! hol cr8 of oranges frm guy sellng sde of rod sez frm FL extra juC. It wll be wld 2 hve them spry when I sht. Nd u here

So Carl's gotten oranges from the side of the road. I can envision how an orange might ooze long after an arrow has pierced its flesh. I can envision stepping away from the wall, the orange-feeders' mouths agape, while *my* orange quivers on its arrow-stalk, the juice leaking down its waxy sides, dripping to the floor. I can envision Carl marching forward and sliding it off, biting right through the bitter skin. I can envision summoning all my strength and wrapping my arms around his thick midsection—lifting him, all of him—and dropping him out a window.

Now Dr. Blau is digging at the back of his hand with a fingernail. Digging so hard that he's drawn blood.

When he sees me looking, he blushes, and his beard bristles like a ridge of fur. He tucks his hand into his armpit, and I wonder what else he's tucked away inside himself.

The bus is stopping. We're on the corner of a busy road that runs into a quiet street. Sycamores line the length of it, so tall I have to crane my neck to see them disappear above my head.

"We're home, Jenny," he says. "It doesn't matter what they all said. I got you home again."

"Whose home?" I say, playing along, still letting myself be guided.

He whispers to me like a father, gently:

"All that matters is you're here."

Optimism: 3
Clarity of Self-Examination: 2
Frustration Over the Efficacy of Rating Systems: 7
Fear: ∅

Dr. Blau guides me to a dark house, the only one on the street without a glowing porch light. A small yard on a hill as smooth as plastic in its untouched coat of snow. No children's footprints, no snowmen, not a single mitten left behind. We walk up a cement stoop that cuts through a hedge that has been devastated beneath a heavy crust of ice. There's a mailbox drooling mail, a puddle of envelopes and papers on the ground.

"Here we go," says Dr. Blau, fiddling with a key.

Instead of being afraid, I'm ashamed of how little of this I knew. Dr. Blau has a house out here in the freezing burbs. For how long? Years it looks like, and I had no idea.

"We're home!" he calls when he pops the door open. He clacks a light switch up and down to no avail—the house is dark—and releases me into the musty air. "This is better than some damn hospital," he says. "Those doctors poking and prodding you all day and night."

Moonlight through the kitchen window makes it bright enough to see. The floor is littered with newspapers still in plastic bags; cobwebs anchor the corners of the sofa to the edges of a rug. In the window itself, a flowerpot holds a gray, filmy substance that hangs in the shape of a deflated philodendron.

"What do you say, Jen? I've got your room all fixed up."

Haven't I walked into the lab early in the morning to catch him bleary-eyed and sipping coffee? Doesn't he walk around in that beaten lab coat like he's wearing his pajamas? How long has it been since he's driven *home*?

"We're back, Hon!" he calls, this time poking his head down the hall. "*Both* of us!" There's a fullness to the way the air does not respond, as if to demonstrate the house is empty—as if to let me know that *Hon* is gone for good.

"Come on," he says, taking me by the hand. The electricity of his excitement enters my palm through his own. We are a circuit, together, and I brighten.

"Okay," I say. "I'm coming."

He opens a door in the hallway, and I say, "Wow," but that's the circuit talking. What I should have said is *Let me go.*

It's a girl's room. A little girl. Frilly riding ribbons hang around the bedposts—satin blues and yellows. There's a soccer trophy on a shelf. On top of the dresser, a purple beret is folded in half, with beaded jewelry strewn behind. There are seashells in a pinch-pot. An umbrella urn filled with peacock feathers. Here she is in pictures. Up on bookshelves with her friends, in ponytails, and I remember. I remember how it was back when I could sprint faster than everyone in my class, never fearing that my lungs might explode. Dr. Blau was right to pick me when he found me in that line at camp. I looked just like her then.

The bed is freshly made, but one of the corners has been pulled back. The puffy pillows are pushed aside and a stuffed monkey, arms wide, invites me between the sheets.

"Wow," the circuit says again.

"It's better here," he says, "with all your stuff."

"It's nice," I say, "yes," and I turn around as if to continue with the tour. But his hand comes to rest on my shoulder, presses down with a weight that belies the frailty of his frame.

"I knew this would happen," he says. "Sweetheart. Listen. I tried to protect you. I couldn't. That's my fault, not yours." From the back of his pocket, he unfolds my checklist, and lays it on the foot of the bed. What I knew a moment ago, I'm not so sure of now. After all, we still have Item 74, Abductophobia: *Fear of Being Kidnapped*, Item 302, Soterioanthrophobia: *Fear of Mistaken Identity*, and Item 214, Autoepistafiliaphobia: *Fear of Being Falsely Identified As Someone Else's Daughter* among the items that have gone untested.

I take the list, and when I do, Dr. Blau steps into the hall and closes the door behind him.

"Dr. Blau?" I say to the door.

I turn the knob, but it doesn't budge. I rattle it. I pound on the wood with my fist.

"Dr. Blau?" I call.

His voice is muffled, but close, like he might be pressing his cheek against the other side. He says, "I knew that bringing you here would work."

Item 183, Athazagoraphobia: Fear of Being Forgotten Or Ignored

Dr. Blau sat me down at the table where sometimes we ate our lunch. We'd order from the Wonder Chicken when the grants were coming in, and that year there'd been a bumper crop.

On a drizzly day like that one, the smell of food would expand to the edges of the room and make us feel that we, too, were warm and delicious. Outside was grayness; the fires had had trouble catching. But in our cave of experimentation, we were safe and dry and free to gorge on oily hunks of meat and broccoli, noodles and water chestnuts the shape of coins.

We sat on stools at opposite ends of the brushed-metal table, and Dr. Blau tucked a napkin in his collar. He cracked his knuckles. The windows were covered with rain.

"Ready?" he asked.

I nodded.

"Your mother . . ."

I had not known what was coming, only the item number on the list, and felt those words, "your mother" immediately touch my spine, right at the base of my skull. It was the kind of crackle a person might experience the fraction of an inch before sticking a paperclip into an outlet. If I pressed my attention too hard into what he was saying, I was at risk of shorting out.

"Yeah?" I said, straining hard to ground myself.

"I'm in touch with her," he said. "I have been for years. She called me right after the hearing. Right after the fu-

neral, actually. That was before she decided to make the break. Now I'm the one who has to call her."

I self-affect rated my fear at Ø, but had to breathe deeply to keep that crackle of heat from spreading from the base of my skull to the rest of my body.

"Where is she?" I asked. I was neglecting the piece of chicken on my fork as it made its journey toward my mouth. It wobbled in the air.

"Christine, you're just supposed to listen to what I have to tell you. Go ahead. Eat. Self-affect rate. This one's easy."

I nodded and tapped my pencil on the phobias list, making little skid-marks on the page between Claustro and Chronomentro.

"Anyway," he said, "at first she was very appreciative of my calls. I think she was pleased that someone was looking after you, though I made it very clear that I was not looking after you—that you were an autonomous adult. But as the years went by, she moved, and then she moved again."

I rated my fear at Ø.

Dr. Blau nodded. When I self-affect rated, he watched my pencil in his peripheral vision. He wasn't nodding at my Ø, but at my participation in the experiment.

"Farther and farther south," he said. "Asheville for a while, then Charleston. I had to track her down each time. She hid herself well. Savannah. Sarasota. Now she's in the Keys. I've called her twice this year. She only answered once."

"What did she say?"

He nodded at my pencil. I rated Ø, again.

"She said 'Stop calling here.' I wasn't surprised. She'd become increasingly hostile toward me. Guilt can wear off, especially in warm weather. I don't know what she thought, maybe that I was tracking her down for money. Really, I was using updates on your health as a Trojan Horse. I wanted to get her talking. People often reveal clues about their genetic makeup unknowingly."

"So you stopped calling?" I said, and then, "The Keys?"

"Oh, I'll try again. It's the only thing that keeps her from forgetting you completely. One day I may need her to come in for blood work. Hints of legal action go a long way toward reopening wherever it is she's stored her child-rearing response."

My hands were shaking on the page so that my 0 came out squiggly. I was only rating fear, ignoring my anger, which was at 10. My confusion at a 9.8. My sense that the world is strange and small and possibly meaningless was off the charts.

Self-Rated Affect Log, 10:53 PM
Optimism: 1
Heated Spine: 6
Wobbliness: 4
Fear: Ø

"I never got my five steps, Jenny. I only got one. I was afraid. I was afraid all the time, the whole time you were leaving, but now I'm afraid *still*. How can you *not* be? You're so close. You're so close to leaving me again."

"Christine," I corrected. I couldn't help it now. I felt like a patient who knew the hypnotist's secret word—that just by saying my name, I could snap him out of it.

"Christine," I said again.

"Yes," he said. "That's the torture, isn't it? That I see you in so many people? That I'll see your hair on some stranger's head? That your nose will be right in the middle of someone else's face?"

"Christine," I said.

I thought I heard him whimper. "Can you just be who you are right now?"

"Okay," I said. "I'll try."

I was brought out here before. Why am I only remembering this now? It was Dr. Blau who brought me. Not to
this house, but to this neighborhood. Yes, definitely, to
this neighborhood. We sat in a coffee shop testing <u>Item
212</u>: *Fear of Other People Being Forgotten Or Ignored.*
Just around the corner, maybe. What else have I been re-
pressing? How hard have I been leaning against the
doors of my precious memory?

Item 212, Othozagoraphobia: *Fear of Other People Being Forgotten Or Ignored*

We'd gone out to get coffee. Dr. Blau was weeping, but it was not unusual for Dr. Blau to weep. For instance, he'd wept during Item 433, Lacrophobia: Fear of Weeping. *But that had been months before. In that coffee shop, each of his eyeballs stirred beneath a bulging lens of tears. They were a different sort of tears. I had my pencil out, and the phobia list in front of me. That was the first day Dr. Blau had not been Dr. Blau.*

"You know what, Jenny," he'd said, sitting across from me with his muffin.

"Christine," I'd said, hovering above my chair. His voice had stopped me from sitting down completely.

"Christine, yes." He was dreamy then, and I felt I could see his thoughts straining like light through a cloud above his head. He said, "I knew a Jenny once. Never mind. You just remind me of her, is all. That's why I made the mistake." He was crying then, yes, but not all of him was gone.

He sat and stared at his muffin, and picked at the wax paper without any real intention of removing it. "And now I might forget her," he continued, as if he couldn't help himself. "In fact, that's probable. Actually, I think I'm forgetting her already."

He was either nodding at my log book or nodding at the muffin. I drew an invisible line down from Other People Being Forgotten to the fear column, and marked a ∅.

"You're still so young, Jenny," he said.

In my head, I said, "Christine," but in that coffee shop I said nothing.

He was making little choking sounds, and if that muffin weren't so resolutely uneaten on the table, I'd have thought a piece of it had lodged down in his throat.

"There's not a day," he choked, "that goes by that I don't check in the journals for something experimental. Some experimental treatment. Just looking, you know. It eats at me. But what good would it do you now?"

I looked down at my paper, and scratched another ∅. I thought: This is interesting.

"You should see your soccer trophy. It's all tarnished from my fingers. Ha. I hold it. I think of you. Your seashell necklace, your beret. But it doesn't bring you back. Nothing brings you back. I cook . . ."

The chokes got stronger, and I knew if he kept on like that, I'd have to alert the staff.

"I cook," he finally got out, "mac and cheese every Thursday night. Isn't that the day we made it? I can't remember. Did you like it? Oh, god. I can't even remember what you liked."

∅, I wrote again in the column beneath <u>Item 212</u>.

Self-Rated Affect Log, 12:03 AM
Anticipation: 8
Sympathy For What I Know: 6
Pity For What I Don't: 8
Fear: Ø

Dr. Blau is down the hall. I can hear him scuffing up the floor with things. I can hear him clanging pots together. 12:03 a.m. Is it Thursday? Is he preparing to boil pasta?

My phone vibrates:

> Hws it hangn? Frgt everythng u evr new re arrows. Makng sum of my own. Ur gonna freak!!! 2 cool Ive bn blowin awy rats!!! 6 alrdy. King pussys back!!!

Alone in Jenny's room, I slide open the top dresser drawer. Neon pink tank tops and neon green tank tops and socks with ankle frills. Eight years old? No. Maybe twelve. When I was twelve I was wearing stuff like this. I was making friends at school. There was so little to be afraid of then. If a girl doesn't cry when the lights go out, her parents aren't worried that she's not responding to fear-stimuli. Her parents just go to sleep.

On the nightstand, Dr. Blau has arranged a menagerie of plastic animals. They surround the lamp so that the cows and rabbits and chickens are fleeing the advances of a lion in mid-roar. Or did Jenny arrange them this way, however many years ago? The lion has its paw raised like a bird dog. I think for a moment that if I had these plastic animals, if I had this nightstand, this lamp, that I *would* have arranged them like this, too. Suddenly,

I'm sad, and when Dr. Blau opens the door, I sit peace-ably on the bed.

"I know you're afraid," he says. He hasn't brought in a plate of mac and cheese, but the whole pot, right off the stove. He's stirring in the cheesy parts with a big wooden spoon.

"I'm not afraid," I say. "See?" I hold up the log and the checklist to show him all my zeros.

He says, "But this was the only way."

My phone buzzes.

Carl's text says:

> Chrissy??? Chriss? Im out of cndy bars pck me up sum. pleeeez. Chris? where r u yur not stll mad re monky? Chrissy? theres a cost 2 evry performnce its alwys wrth it!!! did u c there faces?!!! they were blown. lets tlk. Ill expln 2 u re art and sacrfice

Compassion Due to the Altering of My Schedule: 7
Creative Associations Due to Confinement: 8
Sleepiness: 4
Fear: Ø

The stuffed monkey on Jenny's pillow grins dumbly at me in a mouth stitched with brown yarn. A peeled banana is sewn into its palm. Its eyes are black stones, polished to make them gleam the way that Chicken II's eyes would sometimes gleam.

There's another photo on the bookshelf which at first I hadn't seen. I hadn't seen it because it was placed facing down.

I lift it up.

The frame is made of pieces of driftwood glued together at the corners. The photo is of Jenny, of course. She sits on wooden steps that bisect a composition of leaves and tree bark and knotty-looking roots. It's as if the steps lead through a jungle. She smiles in the way that only a twelve-year-old can smile, when the joy of smelling leaves and tree bark and knotty roots is the totality of her experience. There are holes in the knees of her jeans, feathery white strips of worn fabric. Her t-shirt is crowded with folds, but I make out what it says. *Ruby Brown.* My fingers are weak as hotdogs.I let the picture clatter to the floor.

Back when I'd finally come home, I'd had to walk in from the bus stop. Where had I been? An office park in the Quad Cities? A turbine in Duluth? Wherever it was had been far away. Coming back, I was lost, but it wasn't my sense of direction. I'd gotten the address wrong. Where Dr. Blau had had his lab, they'd built a House of Pancakes. Years had passed, of course, and I'd been up the scaffolds of many buildings. I'd felt the wind in my hair, and been above the morning fog. Up that close to the sun, it was like a flashbulb all the time. My eyes were still adjusting. The world was streaked and blurry.

I'd had to walk halfway across the city to find the new lab. The daycare center and the Wonder Chicken and the apartment complex across the street. Dr. Blau was right there in the middle. I hadn't thought he'd take me back. I hadn't thought he'd forgive me for abandoning him. A study like ours is a great investment of time and money. Experiment after experiment; it all adds up. So where did I get the nerve, coming back? It had started in Cleveland. That's where I'd been. On a window ledge, scraping off a veneer of bird manure, standing in a cage with a squeegee in my belt. How many stories up? Maybe thirty. Wintertime, and I was bundled like the Michelin Man.

In Cleveland, I was with a baldy named Sid Sink, whom everyone just called "Sink." The baldies were the ones who didn't wear hardhats, but Sink was actually losing what he had on top. He let the last wisps of his hair get blasted around in the altitude, without thinking anything of erosion control. Sink had a nose on him, too, a red-veined bulbous thing. It would fill and run with horizontal trails of thick green snot, so that when we stepped back off the lift, it looked like his face had exploded. I shared his trailer for months. We did more than a dozen buildings together, and got them all to sparkle. He was twenty years older than me, and a little ashamed of himself for taking me in, though he treated me like his niece.

"Cleveland's the city that rocks," Sink would say, over and over again. At all times, he had a walkman clipped to his belt, though the headphones stayed wrapped around his neck—as if the pretense of loving music was his civic duty. He'd say, "While you're here you should get out and dance a little."

He drove me to shows in his mother's Thunderbird, which she only let him borrow in exchange for taking her cat to the vet. I'd get out choking from the feline fumes, and the Cleveland air would suddenly be as fresh as Tahoe. But Sink didn't come inside the shows with me. He'd drop me off at the end of the block, and wait until the music ended, sometimes two, three o'clock in the morning. I'd stumble out with the drunkards and the kids shot through with piercings, and see him behind the steering wheel, munching on a burger, reeking of cat and ketchup and grease.

It was about that time that the band *Ruby Brown* was having its regional success. They had a single called "Downtown," which many Clevelanders assumed to be about their own shopping district. When Sink overheard me humming a bar, he bought me a ticket to their show, and when it came time, dropped me off at the basement club. Then he drove around. He ate his burger in the Thunderbird and waited while I danced. But afterwards, when we arrived back at his trailer, I saw that he hadn't been just driving aimlessly through the city while I was in there kicking up my heels. He'd found a cot somewhere, and made it up with sheets, garnished it with some pink and purple pillows. At the foot, he'd laid out the t-shirt he'd bought from one of the curbside vendors.

Up until that point, I'd been sleeping on the floor.

"Well?" he'd said. "What do you think? It's better this way." He was grinning like a clown. His nose seemed to pulse with his resolve. "And I don't want you up on those buildings anymore. It's dangerous. You should be in school. How old are you, anyway? Don't worry. Old Sink's here to set you straight."

I took the shirt and held it up against my chest. It would fit, which was good. When Sink ducked in to use the head, I left everything else behind; that shirt was my only change of clothes.

By the time I found Dr. Blau's new lab, it was evening, and he was sitting at the table with boxes from the Wonder Chicken spread out in front of him. Egg rolls, it looked like, fried rice and seaweed. He was staring at a photo. A driftwood frame, the corners as worried and soft as cloth. If Sink had been certain of my future, Dr. Blau was unsure of who I was; I could see it in the strange quiver of his mouth, though his mustache mostly hid it.

My jeans were torn at the knees in the style of all those Cleveland punks. My t-shirt said *Ruby Brown* across the front.

"Dear God," said Dr. Blau.

I could smell formaldehyde. I thought he must have been embalming something. His eyes were red. He fumbled his hands and knocked the frame from off the table. It lay face down on the floor.

Self Rated Log, 12:46AM
Ability to Recognize Important Things: ?
Sense of Strangeness: 9
Calm: 5
Fear: Ø

Carl's text says:

> Im comng 4u!!! Im yur hero IAM the brave 1 u
> want!!! Wat im doing wll make u afrad 4 life!!!
> Here i com

Dr. Blau says, "I won't deny that this is strange, Jenny.
You being back here with me like this. I'd been under the
impression that once you were gone, you were gone for
good."

I'm sitting on the bed again, and I grab hold of the
post as if bracing for a drop. I'm on the Big Devil in my
mind, and the coming plunge will fill my hair and expand my nostrils.

"I was so scared when I thought I'd lost you. Weren't
you scared, Jenny?"

With my free hand, I rate a Ø.

"Well, I was *terrified*. But maybe you have a point.
Maybe in looking back, it's *always* wrong to be afraid. All
my searching, all my crying, all that bloated pain I felt . .
. and here you are. Here you are again."

My phone buzzes.

Carl's text says:

> Trffcs lite. Im zoooomng. Yd b into it 4 sur. Comng
> 2get u Chris. All my lifs a sugr hi now. Thnks 2 u.

u mke me dream of whats next. Im thinkng hatch-
ets n im so exitd I cn barly breath. The car is
swerving chrissy!!! Im on the shulder rt now!!
That's how mch u mean 2 me. Im rsking lfe and
lmb. Isnt tht wat lve is??? 2 die n nt be scard?

Self-Rated Affect Log 1:13 AM
Anticipation: 5
Shock: Ø
Fear: Ø

Though the door is locked from the outside, Dr. Blau
is out there pounding it with his fists. Instead of turning
the knob, it's the door vs. Dr. Blau, one crashing against
the other.

It opens in a way that can't be good for the longevity
of its hinges.

"You demon!" he yells. His face is red. He holds a
wooden spoon like a weapon, orange cheese still adhering to its edges.

"What?" I say, grabbing the bedpost again. There's a
lamp I can swing if I need to, but I'm a long way off from
that. This is Dr. Blau. He could whip that spoon right
across my face and I'd probably chalk it up to science.
He's never been angry with me before. Am I feeling
shock? No. I'm waiting to see what will happen next. I'm
waiting to see if it will be interesting. If I am anything,
I'm *troubled*, but only a little bit. Or maybe I'm feeling
unrest, clutching the bedpost as I am.

"*You* did this to me," he shouts, pointing the spoon at
my nose. "*You're* the one who torments me all day long."
He raises the spoon behind his ear, but he holds it there.
I brace myself and squint.

Then he drops it to his side, and the spoon is not a weapon. The spoon is just a spoon again.

"Why did you leave me alone with *this*?" he says. "Why did you leave it all here for me to remember?" He goes to the dresser and picks up the seashell necklace. There are a dozen little augers, thin as toothpicks, threaded along a piece of floss.

"You're like a criminal who left behind your finger-prints!" he hollers. "Look! Look at all the evidence!"

He takes the first shell between his thumb and fore-finger, and he crushes it. He crushes a second one, a third. A fourth one disappears. They pop as easily as bubble wrap. He goes up the length of the necklace, crushing all the rest.

I squeeze the bedpost, but I've stopped my wincing.

"You see what you did?" he asks. "Do you understand what you've done to me?"

Dr. Blau is on his hands and knees; the spoon is lost beneath the bed. I unpeel my fingers and place them on his shoulder.

"Get off," he says. "Don't touch me."

I self-affect rate a Ø.

My phone buzzes.

Carl's text says:

> Im going 2 rally shirly n her men. Tgether wll find u chrissy. Wll serch the hol city. Thse guys r good guys whn u get 2 now them. Thy r all intrsted in u n the show. I told thm re hatchets n u shudhve seen ther faces. blown!!!!! this will b big but 1st I hve 2 fnd u chris!! Im lost n yur nt here

Self-Rated Affect Log, 1:28 AM
Disquietude: ∅
Alarm: ∅
Trepidation: ∅
Fear: ∅

Dr. Blau has left me alone again, though I can hear him knocking around with something down the hall. This house is like a failing heart and every distant thump is a surprise. It won't give up, though, not with me inside, my presence like a dispassionate pharmaceutical that keeps it from collapsing.

I squeeze my eyes and fists. I *try*. Maybe a positive rating will break the spell. But I'm honest with the science. I rate another ∅. What I don't want is that moment of struggle—Dr. Blau rushing in with a rope or a bag or a flashing knife. I can't bear to struggle with him like that. I imagine books falling from the shelves. The mirror snapping off its wire and falling to the floor. The bed, groaning on its feet.

I can't bear it. I won't.

Not with Dr. Blau.

I text back to Carl before thinking that I shouldn't:

Im @ Dr. Blaus house in the burbs.

The screen goes gray. The battery is dead.

The struggle doesn't come. Instead, Dr. Blau's eyes look as starved and red as an insomniac's.

"How about this," he says. "I die. If one of us has to leave, it should be me. I've *lived* already. This? What I'm doing now? It's just *going on*. I've had it and I can't get it back. Imagine what I've already had: your mother is sleeping, and little you—you're as pink and wrinkly as a whoopee cushion. *My* little whoopee cushion. I have you against my chest. They've dried your hair, but it still looks wet. You've seen those pictures. Can you imagine it, the wonder of it, how full I must have felt in my own skin? Now imagine me *remembering* what is no longer there. You see? You see the terrible difference? I should be the one to go. You stay. It's your turn to be here with all of this."

Dr. Blau is carrying a mason jar. Inside of it is yellow mist.

"What is it?" I ask.

"You don't recognize it? Ha! Why would you? Why would you know it outside your body?"

"An organ?"

"Your sickness. When they got it out, I saved it. The bastards said I couldn't, but I did."

He holds it up, and I look inside. A collection of swirling spores. Beneath the mist is something moldering. Faint blue and green fur. It could be the crust of a bologna sandwich as easily as a tumor.

"I'll *consume* it," he says. "What does *it* know? A sickness is just a sickness, but the body can be *any* body. The body can be mine."

I think I see him wink. Though maybe it's a spasm.

"That will not be good," I say.

"Good? Ha ha. Remember how you suffered? I'll make an arrangement with you now. You don't want me to suffer, do you?"

"No," I say. "Of course not."

"Well, I suffered just as much as you. More probably. Because when you went away, your suffering ended. While mine just keeps on going. Here's the arrangement: Be good here while I'm gone. I have people I work with, subjects. I don't care about the tests. The world will go on turning without any of my conclusions. I care about the people . . . . The ones I leave behind. Christine—"

"Yes?" I say.

"I have a subject named Christine. She'll think this is all part of what's happening to her. You'll see. She'll start writing on a pad. Tell her that this is not a test. Tell her that this is real."

"Dr. Blau," I say.

"She needs to know that she can feel whatever she wants to feel. That no one's watching her anymore."

I take the wrist of his hand, the one that isn't holding the jar.

"Tell her," he says, "that I'm gone, and that she can be herself again. She can drop the whole charade."

"It's not a charade," I say, shaking him by his wrist.

"Can you imagine the effort? The exhaustion of keeping it up?"

He puts the jar down on the bed and leans into it with his palm, torquing his body so that the lid pops off. Dr. Blau is right. The inside smells as evil as the plague.

I can't help myself. I reach down to my clipboard and rate. My alertness is a 9. My passion, an 8.5. I shake with how little I'm afraid. But I'm tired of being obedient. I'm ready to cut loose and float to some place new.

"Here, here," he says. "So we're in agreement."

He tips the jar of funk up to his mouth, but I am faster.

I unlock it from his grasp. There is no struggle, really. At least I'm spared that.

"*No*," he says, but what can he do? My back is turned. By the time he's grabbed my shoulders and I'm facing him again, I've got it down the hatch. Gone is my sickness. Gone is all of that.

In the future, when my phone has been recharged, I'll see the message Carl has left me. It will be too late, of course.

Im a ball of fire chris. Its nt the arrows burnng its me. I need u 4 fuel. Im fire ur wood. Im spreadng. U dnt realy want 2 stop me becuz u need me 2 lve 2. U need 2 b consumd i know.

Self Rated Affect Log, 1:59 AM?
Curiosity: ?
Jubilation: ?
Discomfort: ?
Fear: ?

A heaviness settles into my chest. It's like a blanket if the blanket were on the inside of my body, pulled up to my chin, covering my heart and lungs. I feel my organs slowing their expansion; I feel them fall asleep. I'm dreaming, and my heart and lungs are dreaming, too. Becoming small. Expanding a little bit less each time.

My vision goes from black to where I'm seeing people. Here I am. A living room, and Laverne is frowning. "Don't point that thing at me," she says, not that I hear her say it. I see her lips move in the shape of the words. The orange-feeders on the sofa release the pithy undersides of orange peels in their S-shaped convexities. Their smiles freeze as I refocus. I am the tip of the arrow. I see it on their faces as I pass by one of them to the next. Though I could veer in their direction and pin one to a sofa cushion, I am sparing them. I fly through the room and see those pictures of Laverne at the bases of snowy mountains. I see the burners on her stove, a spice rack, and then there's me. I stand against the wall. Christine.

There's a cocktail in my hand, rising to my lips. It tilts so sharply that the ice cubes avalanche against my chin, and the liquor runs in channels down my neck. When I lower the glass, there's an olive between my teeth. The room pulls back like a lens retracted. I see Laverne, the whole line of orange-feeders—and I'm streaking toward myself again, racing toward my mouth. It does not flinch or quiver. The me against the wall is as stuck in place as a woman on a poster. Closer and closer. Would it even hurt, this piercing? Would it kill me? Or would it be that slow burn, which is never really pain? The burn of Carl, swiping at my legs, the burn of being left out in the cold, of a house gone up in flames.

I want to hurt this body in front of me, to go in right between the eyes.

But I've been aimed by someone else.

Someone whose aim isn't honest—not as honest as mine would be.

And so my path dips beneath the nose in front of me. The olive grows bigger. I see its orbishness, its sheen. And then it's all I see—what was once an olive is now the bulging curve of my entire vision, deep green, and then a thousand shades of green, and then there is nothing but the truest green, itself, and I'm through and into the wall and everything is black again.

The air inside my dream is fresh, but the air inside my stomach is heavy with the spores of whatever had been left inside that jar. Particles of sickness are colliding with particles of good health.

I wake up, heaving, though nothing inside of me has escaped.

Item 223, Aquaphobia: *Fear of Water and Drowning*

Dr. Blau stood beside the depth finder. He'd been asked a question I hadn't heard, and was answering, "Actually, we don't want to fish at all."

Captain Dave Jorio looked upset. He stood with his arms crossed—a charter boat captain who wore epaulets on his windbreaker and skewered the brim of his hat with fuzzy lures. "Live and let die," I thought I heard him say. The breeze was high and fretful.

"Excuse me?" I said.

Dr. Blau tapped the depth finder's screen with his knuckle. He asked, "Are we above some kind of a shelf?"

"Like, from Wings?" said Captain Dave Jorio. "The only real band Paul McCartney was ever in?"

"Live and let die," I said.

"That's my motto," he said—but if that was true, it was advice that made him frown.

"Now we're talking," said Dr. Blau. "Now we're getting somewhere. Two hundred and forty feet, Christine. 243, 258. Now we're cooking! 326! 333!"

"I'm still at zero," I said, rating again in the log.

Once I'd been up in the air, what was depth to me? The ocean was like a stretch of asphalt. Beneath a layer of asphalt, there are leagues of dirt before you reach the center of the earth. But who's afraid of that? All you feel is road.

"345, 386. We're dropping."

"Actually," said Captain Dave Jorio, "we're still at sea level."

"It's about perception," said Dr. Blau. "It's about understanding just how far you can sink."

Dr. Blau walked across the deck to the rail, where he stood looking out over the ocean. The empty fishing rod holders flashed like quicksilver in the sun. We'd chartered the boat all day, and hadn't dropped a line. "Live and let die," Captain Jorio repeated.

"Come here, Christine." Dr. Blau waved me over. "Come right up to the edge. Perceive this with me."

I walked over to him and perceived. There was a hinge built into the rail, and it opened like a gate.

"Don't," said Captain Jorio, but Dr. Blau already had. He'd put his hand on my back and let me walk right to the edge. Beneath me, the ocean frothed where the boat cut through, and spread like gray and dappled gooseskin. Fear of sharks, fear of squid, fear of gulls, fear of salt—we could have tested for them all . . . and every one of them would have come back negative. But that day we stuck to drowning. When the grant money's good, there's no real point in multitasking.

"Are you sure?" asked Dr. Blau.

"Yes," I said. "Nothing," and his hand lifted from my back so that my lungs opened and I felt the levity of briny air fill my head before he pushed me overboard.

The next thing I saw was the wall of water churning behind the whine of the engine's highest gear. Had there been a struggle? Had Dr. Blau wrested the controls from the captain's hands? Or had this been their plan all along? Was there, in the brochure, a drowning-package I hadn't seen? I floated in the white froth, lumps of wake pushing away from me. What was I supposed to do? I treaded water and watched the boat become smaller; I watched the slate of the sea expand. Finally, the boat disappeared into an egg-white horizon.

After forty-five minutes, my treading was no longer exuberant. My chin had dipped into the water. There was water in my ears.

I did the dead-man's float, feeling like a bubble. I let my head go under and my arms and legs droop, just as I'd been taught at camp. I lifted to take a breath—floated and lifted, floated and lifted. My fear was still a Ø.

I started to swim. The crawl. I was motivated by a sudden hunger. Captain Jorio hadn't fed us on the boat. All around me was the ocean, so I chose a direction and I stuck to it. The sun was overhead.

Was it an hour that I swam? Was it more? Soon, my scapula and humerus were made to feel like flint and steel, so that my shoulders began to spark. Then it spread—my ligaments, dry as rags, were ready to ignite, my tendons like long hanging drapes. It wasn't long before a fire raged in the house that was my body. A house on fire, in the middle of the ocean—I thought the ocean would surely win.

I crawled and crawled, but felt myself begin an ineluctable sink. Finally, when I was completely done, when all my buoyancy had been vanquished, I felt my knees drag against the sand, and a wave carry me onto my stomach. My hair lay beside my face, mixed with grit. Two bare ankles stood in front of me. Dr. Blau's voice was overhead.

"What are you doing?" he asked. "You were just supposed to float."

When the waves came up, the gray hairs on his calves tugged at the anchor of his skin.

"I thought I could make it," I said, my face still in the sand.

"And?" he said.

"Zero."

"Zero now? Or zero then?"

"Zero," I said, "the whole way through."

The waves crashed and sucked me down a couple of inches into the sand. I saw flashes of little white auger shells, thin as toothpicks, the kind a girl might string along a piece of floss to make a necklace.

The beach was noisy, but I could hear him sigh.

"Well," he said, "we can't try again. Not now. Not after I burned that bridge with Captain Whatshisface."

I'm clenching my jaw and feeling dead. How long have I been out? Ten minutes, maybe, tops. A few more blinks and I'm alive again, and Dr. Blau is clamoring through the door like Archimedes.

"Okay!" he says, "Okay. You see! You see? I'm smiling! When was the last time you saw me smile? So maybe you've seen me smile, but not like this. Not like this, Christine. Christine. You're Christine. I accept that now. No mac and cheese for you. You like something else. What was it? I have to go *way* back . . . bologna sandwiches. Years ago. Summer camp. Remember? I remember. We met backstage. Right before that little boy put a knife into your head."

"That's not what happened," I say. "Big Ron carried me off stage." I remember how the earth had trembled beneath me with each piston-smash of his giant legs. I remember the strength of his arms beneath my body. Out and onto that soccer field, where the noise of the crowd was gone. He'd said he loved me. Or maybe . . . no. Something in the back of my mind makes the lines of the memory ripple. It's like raising my eyes and seeing, for the first time, that I've been watching a reflection in the water— that something in truer sharper focus was looming just above.

"Nope." Dr. Blau frowns, but only in reconsidering his correctness. "No, you're wrong. That was when it happened. Interesting. You still don't have it straight. We rushed you to the hospital. We bandaged you up so we could barely see your eyes, but you were conscious. You were wide awake, in fact. That knife went in clean. The little pisser had them sharp as razor blades. You were lucky. When it went in, it scraped your left amygdala and took off all that scar tissue just like stubble. I hooked you up to The Meter, and you were off the charts. Christine. Do you remember? You were so afraid. That knife turned you back *on*. You won't admit it, will you? Even now, after I've gone and told you everything. You won't release yourself."

"No," I say.

"You won't remember that you're fine. That's what's so fascinating. You're fine, Christine. You're fine."

"I'm not your daughter," I say. "I'm not Jenny. Jenny's not coming back."

"I know," he says. "I've accepted that. Didn't you hear me? I've already come to terms. Christine. It's okay. You're feeling something now? Let it come. I've stolen you and trapped you here. Maybe you're afraid."

But I self-affect rate a ∅.

This time, Dr. Blau clutches me by the hand that moves the pencil.

"Look around," he says. "Look at what I've done to you."

Item 6, Taphephobia: *Fear of Being Buried Alive*

We went to the parlor on a Thursday because Dr. Blau thought business would be slow. Barry was at the door, rushing us inside. He was only an apprentice then. We'd greased him with a little grant money.

"This way," he'd said, an apprentice, yes, but already looking like a crypt-keeper. His face was long and sallow, and his bangs were chopped only just above his eyebrows. Both he and his suit were in need of a good steam cleaning. Outside, the sun was shining. I thought, maybe we were doing him a favor, just by getting him to answer the door. His skin was like a plant gone gray inside a closet.

"Hurry," he said.

Dr. Blau slipped more cash into his hand, though there was no one watching, and Barry took us back to where the merchandise was on display. The marble floor squeaked and clacked beneath our shoes. Coffins, like cars in a showroom. The smell of leather and lemon zest. Barry's eyes flitted back and forth, and he made soft, mumbling noises.

"Pick one," he said, at last. "But nothing over there." *He pointed to the side of the room where the coffins gleamed in chrome and mother of pearl. "That's high-end. They'd kill me if I let you in a high-end. They'd literally kill me."*

"Where's the one we discussed?" asked Dr. Blau, and Barry shook a finger at an aluminum tube propped over in the corner.

We walked to it, respectfully, as if someone we knew was already inside. Dr. Blau ran his fingers over the lid.

There was a small glass window where a face might peer out.

"This is typical?" I said.

"Sometimes," Barry told me. "The loved ones like it. Just in case."

"Just in case of what?"

"In case they're not really dead, I guess."

"Not much they could do about it six feet under," said Dr. Blau.

I'd pictured it having clasps, like a briefcase, but of course, it didn't. Barry simply lifted up the lid. Inside, it was upholstered red.

"Hop in," said Dr. Blau.

"Here?"

"Why not? Barry?"

Barry gave a what-the-hell lift of his shoulders.

"We want this to be authentic," said Dr. Blau. He handed me a pen and paper. "Forget the self-affect rating for a while," he said. "When you're in there, just write down what you feel."

"What about the data?" I said, and he looked at me with those sad science-isn't-everything eyes.

He said, "In a subterranean setting, stream-of-consciousness might be best."

I stepped inside, one foot and then the other, standing like I was climbing into another roller coaster car. It wasn't easy lying down, but when I did, I rested my head down on the pillow. It felt as stuffed with corn husks as Carl's homemade mattress.

"Bombs away," said Barry, lowering the lid, and I was covered with a heavy darkness.

Out in the living world, noises were muffled to near silence, and I felt myself borne aloft by the pallbearers they must have always kept well-stocked and hidden. They took me through the doors, and then the light of day came streaming through my face-window. I had just enough room to reach up and tap the glass. That was soundproofed, too. Better for the grieving, I supposed.

Overhead, a row of swishing sycamores came across my view. I looked up into their branches. The day was nice. Funny, I thought, that it took being in a casket to notice the parking lot was ringed with sycamores. "That peeling bark," I remember Antonio saying. "They look sick, right? Sick, sick, sycamore."

Where had I been back then? The Wyman Office Park. Forty-five stories up a building in the Walters Pavilion. Antonio, who had been so sweet. Antonio, who'd try to care for me. What was it with those men? Antonio and Larry and Lance and Rene. Jordan and Bruce and Jamaal. All of them, sweethearts. Norm and Johnny and Tick. Louis, Pepe, Tom and Merv. All of them, gone. Or maybe it was only me, on the move—maybe everyone else had just stayed in place where they were. Poor Wade and Dave and Benny. They should have been nurses or teachers, or project managers, at the very least. They should have been anything but bolters, and wipers, and scrapers of rust. Warm, generous, decent men with gold chains and work boots and gang tattoos, and knives they kept in sheaths hanging from their belts. There should have been a dress code for workers in the air: everyone in white. Men like clouds, just passing.

"How can you tell from up here?" I'd asked Antonio. We'd been blowing around—our buckets on the catwalk—on a sandwich break.

"Not from up here," he'd said, taking my hand. I couldn't convince him that I wasn't afraid of falling. He held onto me like holding onto me was the compassionate thing to do. "Down there I recognized them. Look," he pointed to a scruffy patch of green. "That's oak. Once you know down there, you can find them up here. Maples. Those are easy."

It hadn't been long after that. Some time after we lowered down, he must have blown a gasket. I was halfway to the car before I saw he wasn't with me. He was standing on the platform with his hands pressed against his ears. There was no noise. The sky was empty. They had us working on a Sunday.

"Antonio," I called. He had the only set of keys to get inside the trailer.

I went back, but he just stood there where he was. After a while, he said, "Promise me you aren't pretending. So at least I know it's real."

"It's real," I said.

"So you don't feel it? You don't feel that tightness in your chest when the cart starts to tip? It's like I'm gonna die. I love it. I get all tingly when the wind comes. Isn't that why we do it, Christine? To be this close?"

"No," I said. "Not for me."

There'd been no gradual break in his mood. One day he'd been Antonio. The next, he was like this, shaking his head. Right away, he started sleeping up there, on high. After a week, I had to cover his face in petroleum jelly so the wind wouldn't destroy his skin. By the second week, he couldn't work; the third, he was barely moving.

He'd grab my wrist and pin my palm against his heart. "Feel it?" he'd whisper, and I'd shake my head, saying no to both: that racing near-death feeling or his heartbeat.

Was he afraid of losing whatever he felt inside? Or was he just afraid of me? That my fearlessness might transfer to him?

Poor Antonio. And how many others have faded away? How many others are fading still, at the same time as I've carried on, catching first one bus, and then another? Poor Antonio. Poor Maurice and Renard and Pete. Poor all of them, really.

Barry couldn't get us the hearse, so we used his station wagon with the two rear seats removed. Through the face-window I could see how the upholstery on his ceiling had started to bubble and sag.

I wrote in my notebook: I understand the sadness of all this dying, but I understood all that before. To lose some-one to a box is terrible. But shouldn't that be the end of it?

I wrote, Sad things I don't fear:

Then I underlined it.

<u>Sad things I don't fear:</u>

1. Leaves going from bright red to brown 2. Hearing those trains across town as I'm falling asleep 3. Dr. Blau, when he cries and doesn't think I see

I could tell when we were at the graveyard because the light through my window was leafy again. I was slid out of the trunk and carried to my hole. What I saw was blue sky and bursts of golden light as it bent around the branches, and then the trees disappeared and it was like I was in the sky again, nothing obstructing, forty-five stories high. I imagined Antonio in that box with me. But then I saw a wisp of beard that might have been Dr. Blau's. Was he carrying me? Or had he been ahead, guiding the pall-bearers? When I went down, the dirt walls came up like an elevator shaft. The patch of sky remaining was square, not from the square of my window, but from the deep sides of the grave. I saw the pointed tip of a trowel, retreating. Dirt clods precipitated. A thump against the metal like a snowball against a car. First a pff of impact, then the spread. A scree across my face-window. Soon enough, there was no light. I was alone in my black tube, though if I didn't move, I could have been anywhere. In space, for example. In the upper reaches of the nighttime sky. Or I could have been in the sweet warmth of an office closet— having convinced Antonio to jimmy open a top-story window. And so, I might imagine, I was not alone at all.

In the lab there had been discussion about a headlamp, though at first it didn't fly. "But how will I record?" I'd asked, and Dr. Blau had been forced to concede the point. I switched it on to see my pen and paper. The light made my shoes look muddy, and the red upholstery filled with darkened nooks. Like everyone else, I'd seen the footage of the inside of a colon; it was hard not to imagine the "bowels" of the earth. Dr. Blau had said, "I'm not going to tell you how long we'll leave you down there. It could be hours. It could be a couple days. You'll have no food or water, but you'll most likely survive." He'd paused and done his best impression of a man pinned between guilt and progress. "I can't promise that you won't be buried alive, forever. If that's the case, we'll just pay for the rest of the plot. I've already put down the deposit. Anyway, the grant will cover the rest."

But in the end, they pulled me up in fifteen minutes. They'd only thrown down a smattering of dirt. Barry had his arms crossed, like he'd wanted it done more properly, but Dr. Blau was beaming. He plucked the paper from my hand to look at what I'd written. I'd written a paragraph about digestion. It was based on a memory I had of walking down the Blue Ridge Parkway, thumbing my way to

Ruckersville, when no one was stopping for hitchers. There were blackberry bushes everywhere. I'd followed a trail of bear droppings back into the woods, and seen fresh green shoots growing from their caked and hardened centers—fresh shoots that would soon produce new berries, even though they'd been ravaged and squeezed through those horrible ursine tubes. A bush bearing fruit from a turd.

Buried as I was, I'd written: *How scary is any of that?*

Self-Rated Affect Log, 2:34 AM
Nightmareishness: Ø
Creep: Ø
Foreboding: Ø
Fear: Ø

I shake my wrist free from Dr. Blau, and stand there ready to leave. Something has ended between us, or maybe it's just that the testing is finally over. "You didn't do anything to me," I say, but that only makes him wince. "Look at me," I say. "I'm fine." I say, "I'm absolutely okay."

He stares at me like I've missed his point entirely. "But look at *me*," he says. "*I'm* deranged." He raises his hands above his waist, and makes his fingers dainty, as if he's worried that his touch will leave the print of his transgressions.

"You're not deranged," I say. "I understand. It's all part of the experiment."

"That's not it at all," he says. "Do you hear me? Think back. I'm revealing everything to you. Look," he reaches for the divot on my forehead, scar tissue that I've had since the fire, since I was a different little girl. "That's from the *knife*," he says.

"No," I say. "I tripped. I was running from the flames."

"You were wide awake when we took you to the hospital. You were self-affect rating even then. That was the *first* thing I had you do."

Instead of thinking back, I look to my list of phobias. Item 146, Episetiophobia: *Fear of the Revelation of the Beginning of Things.* As of this moment, it has gone untested. I quickly scan myself. My unease is at a 7, my happiness a 2. My fear is nonexistent.

Dr. Blau just shakes his head. "Listen to me. It seems I don't know how to talk to you anymore. Everything I've tried has been wrong. Or maybe the problem is that I haven't really been trying. All I've done is test. It hasn't been good for either of us. I can see that now."

His phone rings.

"Uh-huh, uh-huh," he says. "Interesting. What do you make of the acceleration of these attacks?" He looks at me with eyebrows meant for the person on the phone. "Uh-huh," he says. "No. No reason to. We're not working like that anymore."

"Who was that?" I ask.

"P.J. Young. Another blaze down near the medical campus."

"Barletta?"

"Mmm."

"Who'd he get?"

"A scientist, actually. Part of their emotional research team. Fifteen-year vet in the field. Apparently, he was poking his subject in the eye with cotton swabs."

"Barletta?"

"The researcher. Fifteen years. Ha! I was poking people with cotton swabs right out of grad school."

"How bad was the fire?"

"The lab," he shakes his head, "is gone. But Barletta got the doc and his subject without a scratch."

"Okay then!" I say. "Let's think about this. You've been in the field your whole *life*. Who else do you know down there? Huh? We can top this, easy. You must know a better doctor doing better research. Let's get ready for when *that guy's* lab goes up in flames."

"I don't think so," says Dr. Blau.

"We'll wait until the fire is hotter, until it's *too* hot, until there's almost no hope of his survival. *That's* when I'll go in."

"I'm sorry, Christine."

"What do you mean you're sorry?"

"This is hard for me. But you have to forget the experiment. Without the experiment, there's nothing to overcome. Right? Forget Barletta. This is *me* being brave. Come here. Let's see what effect this has." He comes at me with his arms wide open—a hug, and I admit, I'm ready to fall right in. But as he closes—his beard crinkling and wavering around a tight-lipped smile—an arrow breaks through the window and sticks into the wall. Its head has been dipped in flame, and fire drips like water from the hole it's made in the drywall. A hat on the bedpost sizzles before it roars and falls apart, its flaming pieces collecting on the blanket. There's a rush like wind in a tunnel and then the bed is blazing. Dr. Blau presses me to the opposite wall. Flames consume the doorway.

Through the popping and shattering comes the faint sound of chimes as window glass tinkles to the floor. It's Carl, pushing away the pieces, and pulling himself up over the pane. He stops halfway through, one leg in, the other one still out in the cold cold world. His bow is stuck. I can hear him grunting.

"Christine," he says, turning his body. He drops the bow around his neck, and uses both his hands to boost himself inside. "I'm here," he pants, "to save you. I bet you weren't expecting *this*."

"How did you find me?" I yell over the beat of the flames.

"I'm a tracker," he says, "by my very nature. And there are things inside your phone. You think you can go anywhere without me knowing?"

"*Home invasion!*" yells Dr. Blau, and wraps a shirt around his hand to pull the glowing handle of the door. A rush of cooler air floods in, but that only lifts the flames up higher. The fire is six feet tall now, maybe seven, lashing the edges of the ceiling in darkened strips.

"Hand her over," Carl says. He's inserting a row of arrowheads between the knuckles of his fist, and Dr. Blau lets go of the doorknob to stand between me and Carl like a wall. Carl rounds his back, and clenches his teeth. The bristles of his beard form a ridge across his cheek.

"Stay away," says Dr. Blau. "You hear me?"

"Let her go. You hear *me*?"

"Carl," I say. "I'm fine. You need to go away."

Carl says, "Don't be brave, Christine."

"I'm not being brave," I say.

The walls are flame. The poster frames have melted, and the first-place medals and plastic animals have burned or fused together somewhere behind the heat. What I see is Carl coming forward. What I feel is Dr. Blau tensing further still. Carl raises the fist with all those arrowheads back behind his ear. It's meant to be the kind of punch that will tear Dr. Blau's face right off, but Dr. Blau is fast—faster than I've ever seen him—and throws his shoulder into Carl's chest. They fall and roll among the smoking floorboards. Carl has lost his arrowheads. I see them flashing at my feet.

"Stop it," I say. "*We need to get out of here,*" as if the fact of their imminent burning will bring them to their senses.

The flames begin to leap so that all I can see is a shimmering wall of heat. This room—with all its dust and desiccated, closed-off memories—flares up like a pile of shavings. I feel a flash against my cheek, and another against the back of my hand. The roar in my ears is too much to bear. The flames crest like a wave that will not crash, and flicker with wild current.

I could be right back there again, when I was a kid, back in our garage. If I listen closely, I might hear him. What was it he said? My father, having just come home from work. The current of flame whipping, just like this. I could see him behind the red shadows—flames like bars that locked him inside a cage. *Can you reach me? Can you pull me out?* I feel myself begin to melt, and try to think that this is interesting. But the heat is blistering, and it wraps around me until there's nothing left to see.

Dr. Blau's fingers are at my feet. I feel them there, like a plea, as they brush against my ankles. Those same fingers have taken me by the shoulder, by the elbow, by the hand. I need to save him, but when I reach down, my arms are ineffectual. They feel like empty tubes of air. My heart is racing, and blood is thumping in my ears. If I could self-affect rate . . . but I know my fingers wouldn't even flex around the pen. The hold goes out of my knees, and I drop down, gasping for breath, and falling backward out the door.

From the hallway, that room is not a room. It's just a door of flames. I should call Officer P.J. Young, and get the FD coming. But my phone is lost somewhere, and dead. A puddle of melted plastic.

There's a tingling in my body that makes a terrible sound, notes beyond the popping of the fire—as if each frenzied cell inside of me is made of finest crystal. They hum, and are ready to break. Are my pupils dilated? Is my color gone? Am I beginning to sweat profusely?

And suddenly, I'm crying. Suddenly, I'm a mess.

"Bye," I gasp. "I'm sorry."

Outside the cold clutches me tightly by the chest. I step out onto a street of pitch-black houses. Where has everyone gone? What am I supposed to do?

I know, I think.

I'll run.

Self-Rated Affect Log, 3:28 AM
Ability to Rate: -
Arms and Legs As Ineffectual Tubes of Air: -
Fear: -
Ability to Rate Fear: -

Self-Rated Affect Log, 3:29 AM
Ability to Rate Coming Back: 2
Arms and Legs Like Ineffectual Tubes of Air: 9
Fear: -
Ability to Rate Fear: -

Self-Rated Affect Log, 3:30 AM
Arms and Legs Like Ineffectual Tubes of Air: 6
Fear: -
Ability to Rate Fear: -

I pump my arms and legs hard, and then harder still, until I can feel them fully again, and I'm steaming like a hot potato tossed out in the snow. Lines in the night sky waver, as the world around me melts and freezes up behind me as I pass.

The shadow of a woman walking her dog becomes a woman walking her dog.

"Do you have a phone?" I shout. "There's an emergency."

"What's happened?" she says.

"A fire!"

"Oh," she says, and looks relieved. "I'm sure it's been reported."

"Look," I say. Behind us is a smudge of smoke against the sky, darker than what the sun has left behind. An orange, tiny, muted sunset—and there is some wonder there—how each little house is capable of this beauty when it burns.

"I just got out," I say.

"Are you hurt?"

"No, but there are people still inside."

She tucks the leash into her armpit and hits some numbers on her phone.

"What's the address?" she says, and I tell her, and I'm running again, even faster now—this sidewalk dutifully shoveled and tossed with salt—fast enough to sweat in earnest, and finally, my forehead is clammy and begins to freeze. I think, *If I stop, I'll die,* and then I think, *I'm lost, and all these houses look the same,* and, *Isn't it interesting how peaceful it is here when a mile south a city is burning, and just behind me a house is burning, when behind any of these doors could be a father who has lost a daughter, whose experiments have lost their meaning, who has kidnapped his subject—accidentally, maybe, but all the same—who awaits an arrow with a flaming tip?*

Barletta. I need to find Barletta and bring him here. It's Barletta Dr. Blau should be testing—and only Barletta who can save him now. That fire's too hot for me, so fine, I guess our experiment is really over. Now we know what it takes to make me freak: it takes Carl and Dr. Blau rolling in the flames. It takes those flames leaping up to touch my skin. It takes a long slow night of Dr. Blau calling me *Jenny*, before he understands it's me again. But not Barletta. For Barletta all of this is easy. Barletta can pull them out.

Ahead, a streetlight floods a corner pink where the salt has dried like an empty tidal pool. It's a bus stop, plowed so wide the crests of snow are waves that bank the houses from the sidewalk. I see men, huddled and waiting there, their voices pulsing in the wind.

One of them is holding a pouch. I can see its silhouette. There are strings attached, or maybe wires. They're fine enough to fit into the tiny holes at the base of my skull. If I can't get Dr. Blau into the pages of a peer-reviewed scientific journal, the least I can do is return his equipment. If that's The Portable, it's worth a fortune. And it has sentimental value, all these years in use.

But the figures at the bus stop are old and stiff, with none of the pliancy of my assailants.

I can see it now; what I thought was a pouch is a bottle. What I thought were wires is nothing at all.

"Hey," I say, slowing down in spite of everything that's happened. "Aren't those things illegal?" Here I am, stopped on the street and freezing, steam rising from my head, chatting with old men again.

"Young lady," one of them says, and that's all it takes. I'm drifting away again, and maybe I'm in love with everything the world can be, with how easy it is to just escape into a conversation. There's something about his voice that reminds me of the wind. He says, "People make incendiary devices out of these things. I found it on the ground. It'd be a crime to leave it there, with all that's going on."

"So you're throwing it away? You aren't going to fill it with flammable liquid and chuck it against a building?"

"Who do I look like to you? Some punk? Lord. This is *my* city here."

"Why not just smash it on the ground?"

"You ever step on glass? Little kids play out here."

"At the bus stop?"

"Hard times for everyone."

I look him square in his trembling, earnest face. The skin around his eyes is as fragile and veined as insect wings.

"My name is Christine Harmon," I say. "What if I were to tell you that I just escaped a kidnapping and a house on fire?"

The old guy doesn't miss a beat. "I'd say I'm not surprised, healthy looking young lady like you. I bet you handled yourself pretty good. I like having young people around this neighborhood. I see you and think that times must be changing for the better, that crime must be going out of style, that a season of compassion and generosity must be slowly creeping in. I'm *glad* you escaped your kidnapping."

I look behind me at the large, dark houses. Everything is quiet. I say, "You don't need someone like me here."

"You'd be surprised what I need," he says. "What we *all* need. Look. I'm finding these bottles on the ground, aren't I? Doesn't that indicate a pernicious rumbling, at the very least? Just below the surface of our quiet community?"

"Or a litter-bug."

"Have it your way," he says, and turns his back to me.

"What if the bus doesn't come?" I say. "You'll freeze to death standing here all night."

He projects his voice away from me, into the faces of his silent friends. He says, "The bus will likely come."

And maybe that's the point. Maybe I was pie-eyed with optimism, agreeing all those years ago to this self-affect rating, to this phobia listing. Maybe I assumed that things would change. But here I am, escaped from a house on fire, freezing on a street corner, where a bus will likely come. What's there to be afraid of, really? The buses stay on schedule while everything around me burns.

"Smoke," I say, pointing to a cloud like an oil stain that spreads on the horizon.

"Snow-cloud, more likely," he says. Is he even looking? His back is to me, still. "Nimbostratus."

But it smells like smoke to me.

<u>Item 4</u>, Pyrophobia: *Fear of Fire*

There was a year the grants came in faster than Dr. Blau could apply for them, more money than we knew what to do with. I remember lunch after lunch from The Wonder Chicken. Chef specials and combination platters, too, not just skimping à la carte. Those delicious dipping egg rolls as appetizers. I should have sensed something was on its way. Dr. Blau was getting thinner. I have to squeeze my eyes and really concentrate to remember that he was once a robust man.

What must I have been saying in my sleep that first go-round? He had me on a cot in the back, hooked up to The Meter. It was just a cinder block closet, but he'd dolled it up with posters of the Hot Steppers and Renaissance Boyz. Maybe Jenny had liked them. Or maybe he'd only thought she would.

The first morning, I'd woken to him sitting at the foot of my bed. He'd been taking notes.

"We're going to do a fire," he'd said.

"What kind of fire?" I asked him, and The Meter blipped its steady rhythm.

"Why, are you feeling something?"

"No," I said. I was just a child, really. How could I tell him that what I felt was strange.

"A controlled fire, though I shouldn't be telling you that. I've already contacted the Department. They're in favor. They like to use them as training exercises. We'll actually be helping them out."

"Where?" I asked.

"Garage?" he said, slowly, watching my eyes for pupil-dilation.

"Oh," I said.

"Something about a garage?"

"You know that's where it happened."

"Right. Well. I've got a couple contractors on retainer. They'll bend over backwards if the figures are right. You know the empty lot where there used to be a Mighty Fresh? We'll stage it there. If we go through the Department, we can tap into eminent domain. All we have to do is set up the construction. The Department takes care of all the ashes. Christine, this might be tough on you."

"It won't be tough," I said.

"But, if it is—"

"It won't be."

"I want you to self-affect rate. There will be a lot of commotion—saws and electric drills and those concrete pouring trucks. I know how you like to get your hands dirty, how you like to be involved. That's fine. I just don't want you to forget to self-affect rate."

"Do I ever forget to self-affect rate?" An anger sparked inside me that I didn't want to cool.

"No," said Dr. Blau. "You never forget to rate ... What do you think will happen if you forget?"

"I'm not afraid of forgetting," I said, as the burn in my stomach started to catch.

Dr. Blau had me talk to the contractors and all the guys down at the Department. They wanted to know the specifications, but all I could see when I tried to remember were the flames.

"There should be fire," I told them, and they said, "Yeah, we know. That's kind of the whole idea."

"Okay," I said, and took another breath. I made sure Dr. Blau was out of sight, around the corner, helping the cement truck in the back—I don't know why. I squeezed my eyes, and said, "Hold on. I have to think about what happened before."

I stood there and really thought about it, until it all started coming back. I told them about the garage's ceiling, how it had dark beams with wires slung across. I told them about the automatic door, how it would catch and stop so I could walk beneath, the wisps of my eight-year-old hair just grazing the bottom panel. I told them about the giant springs that pulled the door back along its tracks, how my father had told me never to stand beneath them—that if they ever snapped, pieces of metal would fly at me fast as bullets. I told all those builders and firemen—though they hadn't asked—how interesting I'd thought that was, how I would stand there until my parents came home from work, wondering if a bullet wound feel hot—if it would warm my entire body.

"There was a bucket of rags," I told them. "That's where everything started."

"Circuitry spark?" one of them asked.

And I said,"Yes," without even thinking.

I told them, "Right above the bucket, my father had a workbench. It was just plywood, I think. It caught really fast."

I watched them bring in plywood, and plunk down their circular saws. I watched them watch me as I nodded, yes, yes, that's right—you're cutting the length just right, and as they fastened the whole thing onto sawhorses, just as my father had done it years before. I watched them watch me as I said, "A little lower. Just a little. My dad was kind of short," and just like that I was thinking about my father, who really had been kind of short, though until I'd said it, had never seemed so in my memory. And then I watched as everything changed—that is, changed into the perspective of me, that day, a fourteen-year-old girl who was used to skipping school—and I asked that they raise the beams a little higher, and paint the door a brighter shade of white. I asked that they stain the cement floor with a smattering of oil.

"There should be a cardboard box up there, filled with sweaters, but don't close it very well. Try to make it like you could never really figure out how to close a cardboard box correctly. That should be in direct line with the flames. Can you make those flames come out blue? A light, almost aquamarine color. I think there was a mohair sweater inside. Or maybe just that thick rag wool. Over there, a pile of wrapping paper tubes. Old. Never taken out of their plastic."

"It'll be hard to get old," they told me. "Shouldn't matter, though. New will burn the same."

I sent them out for a vacuum cleaner, and we experimented with burning different bags. Everyone was game. One we filled with lint from a dryer. One we filled with cotton balls. Both took a moment to catch, and then erupted into flame.

"It should just sizzle," I said. "It isn't right. I want it to get very hot, but in the way a magazine cover won't catch but blacken. I want it to blacken the whole way up until there's nothing left but ash."

"Ma'am," they said. "This is synthetic material; it's gonna flame."

They ended up packing it tightly with wet leaves. It smoked too much, but it would have to do.

We positioned the cans of solvent on the shelves, and my father's hat collection in the rafters. Cheap fedoras and floppy wide-brims that he would buy and never wear. We put the extra table in the rafters, its oak-leaf stacked like a three-hour-log on top of all of that kindling.

Dr. Blau was at my side. I hadn't seen him come, and when he put his hand on my shoulder I jumped a little; he was not my father—my father whose headlights coming home would startle me when—as an eight year-old girl—I would stand beneath the garage door, waiting to be shot with springs.

"Oh," I said. "Hello."

Dr. Blau was grinning, but he wasn't grinning at me. His eyes were sweeping the garage. "Glorious," he exclaimed, "what a team like this can do." Then he looked at me to gauge my own appraisal. He nodded as if I'd spoken. He said, "You'll stand right here, right where you are, and then you'll push the button to open the door and the whole thing will go kablooey. You won't be one-hundred percent safe, of course. I can't guarantee you that. This will be extremely dangerous and there's a chance that you might die. One of the fiery beams may very well come crashing down on your head."

"Oh," I said again. There was something clattering inside me like a chunk of plastic in a fan. I felt its indiscriminate landings and knockings-about, and knew it would be insignificant until it lodged somewhere vital, shutting down the system and letting the heat settle over me again.

"What was here?" asked Dr. Blau.

He hadn't sensed the clattering inside of me, and so of course, the clattering meant nothing to him. He asked, "Can you remember?"

"A sewing dummy," I said. "My mom liked to make her own clothes. There was always a sheet over it."

"A sheet over it?" he said. "Perfect!"

"She used to dress it up," I said. Strangely, I felt I was still speaking to the group of firefighters—a swirl of busy strangers—instead of to this man I knew. "She would put a hat and a coat on it. It freaked my father out every time he came out here for his tools, so he made her cover it up."

"Perfect, perfect," said Dr. Blau. "That's where I'll be. I'll be standing right there with a sheet over my head. Oh. Damn. I shouldn't have told you that. Well. I may or may not be standing over there. Now I'm not so sure. It may just be the dummy."

Eventually, they dressed me up in a semi-flame-retardant suit. Dr. Blau wore one, too, beneath the sheet. He stood there perfectly still. Before we started, he said to me, "Try to remember just what it was you were thinking that afternoon. Then think that way again."

"This is fear of fire," I said, "not fear of a particular fire."

"Oh, come on, Christine," he said. "You can see what we're doing here."

So I stood there on the masking-taped X the firemen had blocked on the floor, thinking about that Chinese menu, how the letters had shifted their colors like a time-lapse of trees in autumn—green to yellow to orangey-red. How soon the menu was dead, and ash was fluttering in the afternoon breeze. I thought about how just before it was gone completely, I'd touched that flame to a rolled-up newspaper, and then to another. How the flame was re-born each time in blossom, how it collapsed on itself and I wasn't afraid.

"Like this, ma'am?" one of the firemen asked. He looked vaguely familiar. He knelt at the bucket of rags. "This is whereabouts it started?"

He flicked his lighter, but the rags wouldn't catch. He had to dip them in kerosene.

But when they went up, they thrummed in the bucket like a jet engine—a canister of concentrated, propulsive flame.

I stood and watched. My hands were at my sides. The fire was not yet large enough to warm me.

"Affect-rate!" hissed Dr. Blau from beneath his sheet.

I raised my clipboard. I knew there were all manner of phobias, and phobic responses listed there, but for some reason the letters squirmed around like bugs. I reached down and wrote a big fat Ø next to one of them.

"Really?" said the sheet. "Concentrate . . . concentrate on what's happening all around you."

I concentrated on the flames as they spread and flattened on the underside of my father's workbench, blackening it at first, but then bursting through. I concentrated on their red hot center—the source beneath, that bucket of rags—and how they lolled yellowish at the corners of the plywood, and fell to the floor like hunks of goo. I concentrated on their acceleration, how quickly they ate up all those sweaters—how the folded squares of wool became floating ghosts of pale white heat, the fire luxuriating in their shape for just a moment, before agitating and reaching higher, spreading to the wall itself, adhering in patchy columns, and climbing still.

When I tried to self-affect rate, I could no longer tell if the squirming was coming from the letters, or from somewhere deep inside my body. Was I standing still, or rattling around? I managed a shaky Ø, maybe on the page, maybe slightly off.

Dr. Blau didn't notice. His sheet was moving, too.

When the hats caught, they went up like Roman candles, each a prolonged sizzle of sparks. The Department must have paid too much for them; all those years ago, my father's collection of cheapos had gone up quickly. The rolls of wrapping paper went next, the plastic bubbling and receding in tubes of drooping flame. There were flames in the rafters, too, pouring over that dining table like an unstoppable spill of red, fiery liquid. It shot forward in horizontal fingers, sucking the air out of the garage, sucking it from my chest. Outside, I heard the thump of hose-water beating on the siding. Rookies, probably, still going through their training. They'd opened up too early.

With the sheet over his head, Dr. Blau was shaking like he was clothes-pinned to a line. Could he see me? I self-rated another Ø.

"Go," I said to him. "Get yourself out of here." But he stood there and continued his trembling.

Again, I notched a Ø. I was seeing lines in the spaces between the flames, where each flame refrained from burning. Blackness twisted there. The lines adhered; they broke apart.

"Dr. Blau?" I said, but the flames roared too loud for him to hear me.

And then I saw that it was not Dr. Blau. Between the lines of flame was my father, wrapped in shimmering heat. His silhouette bled and rejoined itself in front of the automatic door.

He'd come back again to find me. "Dad?" I called to him.

I felt a tap on my shoulder and my heart grasped desperately at whatever it was clutching.

"Rate."

It was Dr. Blau.

"Rate once more and we get the hell out of here," he said.

The vision of my father was gone, and flames swirled cyclonically overhead. The crash of hose-water was somewhere far away. I held up my pad and rated another Ø. There was no category for what I'd seen. If I lied, it was only an omission.

"Come on," he said, and pulled me outside, where the firemen had constructed a tent out of flame-resistant fabric. The roar was still in my ears though, and the tips of my hair had singed. I self-affect rated so fast I thought I'd make the paper smoke—but the paper was already smoking.

Again and again, I held up the log and rated.

He'd been there, between the flames, right in front of me. There with his arms outstretched, begging me to come.

My father.

This was the experiment that forced us to start all over again—all the way back to the beginning. Because without my notes, what was there? I turned to face the flames once more, and chucked the log-book in.

Outside the tent, everyone was soaking wet. There'd been a problem with the training, vis-à-vis hose control. Dr. Blau's lips were purple behind the bristles of his beard. He was shivering.

"It's gone?" he was asking me, incredulous. "You lost it?"

"I'm sorry," I said.

He bent over and put his hands on his knees as though he'd suffered a punch to the stomach.

"Well," he said, wincing a little. "Can you remember? How you rated?"

"You saw how I rated."

"Yes, but I didn't see it all. There was more that you put down."

I looked at him, ashamed—but kept myself from cracking. Cracking would have sent a shower of sparks flying out of my chest. "It was all in the log," I said. "Now . . . I don't know. I don't remember. Everything was in the log. It all burnt up so fast."

"But if you had to . . ." he said. "If you were forced to remember . . ." One of the firemen came over with a pinched expression and a tackle box full of cold packs.

"You okay?" he asked.

"I don't know," I said.

But of course I knew exactly how I was.

Self-Rated Affect Log, 4:40 AM
Pulse-acceleration: 7
Ability to Rate My Own Fear: 5
Clarity of Thinking as it Relates to My Ability To Rate
My Own Fear: 10
Fear:
Ability to Write Numbers: 2

Though it's dark, the sky is ready to burst its seams with
the light of day. One of those clouds is different, and
that's the one I'm running for. It swells from a funnel
point and churns gray with pieces of ash.

Barletta will be there, maneuvering among the
flames.

So, I run toward Barletta.

The further I get into the city, the more daydreamy
the tracks of the snowplows become. I see the evidence
of their work in the dirty berms that come and go without
a pattern, or maybe they're patterns of chaos I don't yet
understand. The sidewalk is impassable, six inches of
snow at least, topped with a crust of ice. For a mile or so,
I run in the street. Nighttime trucks buzz me and coat
my legs in slush. Then, the bus. It comes so close I feel its
wind push against my body, and then it passes, and
there's a long period of quiet in which the hum of streetlights is the only sound I hear.

I run past sandstone churches—brown and gray and
glittering. Huber Memorial with its red front doors like
lurid lips squeezed shut. A faint amber light from the
backs of Sun Chinese and the HiValu Thrift Store.
Wozi's Lounge of Jazz Music sits silent. Big Joe's Deli.
The Double Blessing Hair Studio. Then rowhouses and

single-family clapboards cast in shadows and peeling paint. I sprint and pass them all, feeling a strange warm draft of air coming up from the city's guts, buoying everything on the street—and buoying *me* above everything else. I'm an impossible stream of bubbles in this unrelenting block of ice. I pass a mural: MLK, and a woman lifting up her child. The walls are chipped, and dead patches of concrete block show through the brilliant color.

The smoke begins to pancake out, and I know I'm almost there. In the air, I can taste the char of wood and plaster and brick that tastes like the char of anything else—like burnt flakes of pork or duck or paper. Everything disintegrating into bitterness.

Then there's police tape and a fire engine blocking off the street. Folds of hose are caked in grit, and no one gawks because it's late, and anyway, all of it has happened so many times before. *Nothing to see here.* People stay inside where it's warm, fooling themselves that their walls can keep them safe. On the street, there are puddles beneath the smoke. It's all turning to ice. Everything is slick.

I put my hands on my knees and gasp. My hair is wet and cold. There's a pressure on my back. Maybe I'm collapsing. But no. It's Officer P.J. Young, his hand between my shoulder blades.

"Christine," he says. "You got here quick. The doc's already at the hospital."

"What?" I say, not hearing him, my ears still clogged with my swollen heartbeat. "Where's Barletta? I need to find Barletta now."

"Barletta's gone. He saved these folks, though," and he waves a hand across the street where a couple sits on their stoop beneath a blanket.

"What do you mean *gone*?" I say, though I know exactly what he means: Barletta has run away again.

"That man does not stick around. What can I say?" He hangs his face in apology. "Why don't you talk to the survivors?"

I walk across the street to the blanket-people, as they take their deep and jagged breaths.

One of them says, "You're gonna catch cold *again*, Miss. How many times do we have to warm you up? What'd you do with that jacket now?"

"Oh," I say, and it's my embarrassment that warms me. "Hello."

"Look," the other woman says, and I see them more clearly, crushed together beneath the blanket and left on this inky depression of concrete. She looks up and points. "Snow's coming."

I look up, too, but if these are snow clouds, they've mingled with the smoke. A block away, I can't see buildings anymore, just a gray slate pushing forward.

"You saw him?" I ask. "Barletta?"

"Bar-*who*?"

"The man who saved you."

"Not a hair on that man's head. Shiny, you know?"

"Did you talk to him?"

"Oh *sure*. You don't just leave your house with a man before talking to him."

"Did he say anything about . . ."

"About what, Miss?"

And now I can't resist—though I know that time is wasting. "About how it *felt*?"

"I imagine it felt hot. It was really hot in there."

"Yes, but . . . he didn't even *know* you."

"Oh, I expect a man like that knows something. We were in the bathtub. He knew just where to find us."

The other lady says, "That's where it was coolest, in the bathtub."

"I'm talking about something else, though," I say. "He didn't seem afraid?"

"Afraid? We were all afraid."

I think back to my symptoms chart, the chart that Dr. Blau so many times has had me recite before my meals. "Did his voice quaver?" I ask. "Did his pupils dilate? Did you see him sweat? Did he look faint? Did he lose his coloration? Do you think he'd have described his arms and legs as feeling like ineffectual tubes of air?"

"Tubes of air? Miss, he just said, 'C'mon, ladies, time to get on up out of the tub.'"

"That's right. He said, 'Bath time's over.'"

"And that was enough?" I ask. "You just went with him?"

"You see what's left of the house over there? There was nowhere left to go."

I wrap my arms around my body to quell my coming shivers. The wall of smoke and cloud is getting closer.

"Did you see which way he *went*?" I ask, and both of them shake their heads.

And then I can't hear them any more. All I hear is the voice of Officer P.J. Young, the way he'd said, *The doc's already at the hospital*—and it's as if the words had evaporated before reaching my ears, and only now are raining down on me.

I hurry back across the street to where P.J. Young is standing.

"Yeah," he confirms. "At the hospital." He looks unfazed. In his line of work, people must end up in the hospital every day. "I got it on the radio. They took him there okay, but he was in pretty rough shape. They had trouble getting the ambo to the house with all the ice."

"He was burned?"

"Burned? No. Guy shot him in the chest with an arrow."

I see it as it must have happened. Carl running his hands along the burning floorboards to find his bow and quiver, nocking one back and letting it fly.

"The hospital," I say. "I have to go."

"You don't have a jacket," says P.J. Young, though something sly has crept into his voice. "You should come with me."

"No," I say, and start to walk, but he has me by the arm. He can't keep Barletta in one place, but he sure holds onto me. I try to shake free, but he has years of experience keeping people from shaking free. He gets me tight and keeps his face removed from the whipping of my hair. "Christine," he says. "Be still!"

I have to hunch all the way over in the slush and perform a forward roll to unhook myself from him. Then I start to run.

"Christine!" he calls, but by then I'm already gone.

Self-Rated Affect Log, 5:12 AM
Awareness of body shivers: 9
Understanding of the Relationship Between the World's
Meteorological Shifts and the Dwarfing of Human
Experience: 9
Sadness: 8.5
Sadness: 10
Fear:

The wall of gray is on me now. The old man was right—
they're clouds—maybe even nimbostratus—too fat with
snow to remain suspended off the ground. They roll in
like a fog, but with a speed that nearly knocks me over.

Down the street, I can't see ten feet in front of me,
and I stand there clutching the frozen pole of a stop sign.
In another second, I can't see the pole. "I'm going to the
hospital," I say out loud. "I *am getting myself* to the hospital." I take another step forward, and then another.
The snow begins to sting my face, my neck, my fingers.
For a moment, it seems to be coming from below, as if the
world is upside down, and I don't know where I am.

The hospital must be blocks from here. Or maybe it's
blocks in the other direction. I listen. I listen for another
call, another *Christine!* from P.J. Young, but P.J. Young is
saving himself somewhere. There's a hiss in my ears—the
hiss of the snow, and of small pieces of zinging ice. It's
the hiss of a wound, too—the way skin might accept the
hot tip of something sharp. An arrow in the chest, for example. I can feel it from where I am, his life steaming out
of him as if from a raging kettle. I concentrate and let the
feeling burn me up. If I think about it hard enough, I
might just melt this mess around me. I might just set my-

self on fire. "I am going to the hospital," I say, but the wind is blowing me around, and I take tiny, careful steps toward nothing.

I shiver again, but it's not from cold. My heart squeezes rough-edged bolts of blood through my body, scraping channels into all my gory inner strangeness so that my breath comes haltingly again.

I am going to sit. I am going to sit right here because there's nowhere else to sit.

I sit.

I push my face between my knees to keep the wind off of my cheeks. There is nothing left to see. The hospital is gone. At least, it's gone for me. Dr. Blau will lose his life from a hole in his chest, and I'll sit here and simply freeze.

I take the pen from my pocket, and try to rate, but as I do, something grabs my arm. Someone is lifting me up.

The Portable is gone, but I bet that all the way across town—in that empty, forsaken lab—the needles are really jumping. All this time, I didn't need to talk to him—all I needed was to hold his hand.

Barletta has come to rescue *me*.

I can envision it all—everything that's led him to this moment—the practice he's had across the city. I see him pulling a husband and wife from beneath a falling ceiling. They've sucked down too much smoke to stand. He gets the husband under the arms to take him down the fire escape, but it's not so easy with the wife. A bouquet of dried hydrangeas has caught fire near the window. He has to knock it over with his sleeve. He has to pound his sleeve against the carpet to keep it from igniting.

I see the building on Hammeker Street—a flaming bottle arcing up and over parking spaces like the opening

233

salvo of a fireworks display—one sulfuric dot that whispers up, up, up, and then cracks the night wide open. All that office paper, those pencils—an inferno, and I see Barletta charging up the stairs where the walls are breathing fire. He has to wrap his shirt around his face.

There's a woman there.

He pulls her out.

How did he know just where to find her? How does he know just how to save me now? Maybe he's lived it all before. Or maybe he lives in a perfect dream, and in that dream he's normal. It's only down here that he lifts up full-grown men like they're little children, with an arm around their waists. It's only down here that frantic dogs go calm when they feel him coming, where a grandma finds the strength to lift herself and wrap her arms around his neck.

It's only down here that he pulls me from the snow.

"Hey," I say. "I found you."

"Please," he says, his voice both unsteady and sharp—the twang of a saw blade warbling. If I was freezing in a daydream before, Barletta has cut me loose from it.

"Help me," he says, his voice right in my ear. "Please help me get out of this."

I'm standing now, my hand in his, the snow filling up my eyes and ears and nostrils.

"I can't see," he says. "I'm lost," and I say, "I can't see anything, either."

His teeth are chattering, dicing up his words. "O-oh gosh," he says. "Oh-oh-oh gosh."

I'm confused.

"You're afraid?" I say. "It's just a little storm."

Barletta shakes his head. He whimpers. Finally, he speaks.

"I'm always afraid. All the time. I have no one to talk to about this. You won't leave me here alone, will you?"

"But the fires. You've saved all those people."

"How do you know that? How do you know about me? Who sent you here?"

"You're famous," I say. "A hero."

"No," he says. "I have a condition."

"Me, too," I say, though he doesn't seem to hear. His lips are moving as if to complete some final, whimpering admission.

Then he says, "If you live in fear, it's not worth living. Isn't that what people say?"

"Why do you do it?"

He grabs me at the collar. "Lady," he says. "Are you crazy? We're trapped in a blizzard out here."

"Just tell me, please."

He releases me and I fall back to the sidewalk. I'm just a few feet away, but in the swirling snow, I can hardly see his face.

"I'm going to die in a terrible storm," he says, "and what am I doing? Answering some lady's questions."

"That's right," I say. "Go on."

"I don't know," he says. "I just can't stop. I get fixated on a thing, and I have to do it better."

"What kind of things?"

"What's it matter?"

"Come on, Barletta."

Through the snow, I can feel him staring back at me. "How do you know my name?" he asks. "Did those Channel 4 people send you?"

"Tell me what kinds of things."

"There's supposed to be a woman—that's what the papers say. She rescues people all the time. Whenever I hear about her, something takes hold of me. It grabs me, like, out of my control. Whatever she saves, I have to save it better. I can't stop. I hate it. I'm so scared, that being scared's the only thing I ever am. When I hear about her on TV, I stop whatever I'm doing—cutting a steak or vacuuming, whatever—and I have to do it, too. And then the next time I cut a steak or vacuum, I'm afraid it will happen again. I had to get rid of my TV, but do you know how hard it is not to hear the news? And now this freaking storm. Please. Lady. Just help me."

For a moment, the wind subsides, and I can see his eyeballs twitching in his skull. He should be back at home, cuddled up in a snow-day blanket. It's only his compulsive, ungovernable body that has brought him out to me. His mind is running for cover.

I think I know him, then.

"Did they used to call you Roger?" I ask.

"What?" he says, raising himself a little. "No one calls me that anymore."

If I could write a Free Association Memory Entry right now, it would be about Barletta as a boy, picking up those knives in the woods before Paul tackled him to the ground. And it would be about that masked man at Laverne's party, the one who'd out-Carled Carl, the same who'd broken into that toad exhibit—the man who used to be that little boy who couldn't help but mimic, even if it meant walking in front of a dining hall full of campers, just to split his pants. The boy who I'd egged on.

"I *know* you," I say. "It's Christine. Christine Harmon. We went to camp together."

"What?" he says, and then he turns away. He says, "I went to a lot of camps."

"This camp was on a lake."

236

"Every camp is on a lake."

"You tried to throw knives at me in the woods. It didn't work. Remember? You spent a week in the infirmary."

"Oh," he says. "Yeah. Maybe I do remember you."

"You still can't help it, huh?" But the wind picks up and I can't hear how he responds.

I take him along against the blinding storm, and finally feel the stone wall of a building, a glass window. I follow its contours to an awning. The fabric overhead is thumping in the wind. We stand there huddled on the stoop, seeing nothing but each other—or at least I'm seeing him, because Barletta has his eyes squeezed shut. I tell myself the hiss of the snow is not the hiss of something essential escaping irretrievably into the world. And I know it now, what it was they loved up there—forty, fifty, sixty stories in the sky. All those men. Rick and Justin and Frank and Phil. Antonio and all the rest, surrounded by the never-ending suck of life outside their bodies. And I know why I loved it, too. When it blew, the only thing to do was to let go of a railing, unclasp a safety belt, take your helmet off and let your hair stream in the wind. What was there to fear when everything just kept on blowing? Even down here—even *now*—it seems that life will still go on.

"I was trying to get to the hospital," I say, and hear him mumble something unintelligible in response. "Funny," I say. "I thought that you could help."

And then I remember my *own* ride to the hospital. All those years ago at camp. It comes back to me like the clouds have parted, and the obfuscation of this many-years storm has passed. I see my life—just as Dr. Blau had said it was—laid out before me once again. The way that knife had gone through and scraped me clean—the blood, and the race of my heart, those terrible back roads, the way we'd clattered together in the back of that medical van. I'd been at camp a month, and my parents were a thousand miles away, comfortable in their own home, eating dinner. What did they know of my speeding toward a hospital? Someone was holding compresses to the front and back of my head, and Dr. Blau—Oh, Dr. Blau—forgetting his experiments and all his training, was kneeling in front of me, remembering something else.

And now I remember it, too. All of it. The way it really was.

"Christine," I hear him saying.

I feel his hand, as it was, on my shoulder. I feel his hand taking hold of mine. He smiles, and every hair on his face is a kindness.

"Christine," he says, and he's a father, once again. "I'm here. It's okay. Don't be afraid."

Other titles from Malarkey Books

Faith, Itoro Bassey
Music Is Over!, Ben Arzate
Toadstones, Eric Williams
It Came from the Swamp, edited by Joey Poole
White People on Vacation, Alex Miller
Your Favorite Poet, Leigh Chadwick
Thunder from a Clear Blue Sky, Justin Bryant
Deliver Thy Pigs, Joey Hedger
Guess What's Different, Susan Triemert
What I Thought of Ain't Funny,
edited by Caroljean Gavin
Un-ruined, Roger Vaillancourt
Pontoon, a literary journal
Man in a Cage, Patrick Nevins
Don Bronco's (Working Title) Shell, Donald Ryan
*The Life of the Party Is Harder to Find Until You're the
Last one Around*, Adrian Sobol
Forest of Borders, Nicholas Grider

CPSIA information can be obtained
at www.ICGtesting.com
Printed in the USA
BVHW080954240922
647547BV00002B/15

9 781087 896397